GRAPES, GANACHE AND GUILT

A CHOCOLATE CENTERED COZY MYSTERY

CINDY BELL

CONTENTS

Chapter 1 — 1

Chapter 2 — 13

Chapter 3 — 25

Chapter 4 — 33

Chapter 5 — 49

Chapter 6 — 61

Chapter 7 — 73

Chapter 8 — 83

Chapter 9 — 95

Chapter 10 — 111

Chapter 11 — 123

Chapter 12 — 133

Chapter 13 — 145

Chapter 14 — 157

Chapter 15 — 171

Chapter 16 — 183

Chapter 17 — 197

Chapter 18 — 213

Whipped Chocolate Ganache Cake Recipe — 221

Also by Cindy Bell — 225

About the Author — 231

ISBN: 9798655481657

CHAPTER 1

"I have to hurry, ladies, I'm meeting Luke for dinner tonight." Ally Sweet smiled as she collected a few small plates from the counter in front of Mrs. Bing, Mrs. Cale and Mrs. White.

"Is that what you're wearing to dinner?" Mrs. White scrunched up her nose as she looked over Ally's jeans and plain, white blouse.

"Yes?" Ally pulled off her apron and set it on the hook not far from the cash register. "Why, is there something wrong with it?"

"Not wrong exactly." Mrs. Bing pursed her lips as she cast her eyes toward Mrs. White, and then Mrs. Cale.

"Since when are you three the fashion police?"

Ally grinned at the trio of women huddled around the front counter of her grandmother's chocolate shop, Charlotte's Chocolate Heaven. Mrs. Bing, Mrs. White, and Mrs. Cale were regulars at the shop, and had been since Ally was just a young girl. She'd grown up with them acting as extra grandmothers, on hand to dish out advice, or gossip about their small town, at a moment's notice.

"I wouldn't say we're the fashion police." Mrs. Cale popped a candy from the box she'd purchased into her mouth. The three ladies had finished all of the samples. "Just concerned friends."

"Concerned about what?" Ally narrowed her eyes as she looked between them. She could always tell when they were up to something. Mrs. Cale's nose would twitch, Mrs. White's voice became even more regal, and Mrs. Bing's cheeks turned bright red.

"Well, the restaurant he's taking you to, it's quite fancy, the nicest in all of Blue River." Mrs. White huffed, and her voice took on a faint English accent. "It is only proper to dress appropriately for the evening."

"Oh yes, and Luke has gone to all of this trouble to arrange a special night for you, you wouldn't want him to think that you didn't want to go to any special effort to please him, would you?" Mrs. Bing batted her lashes against her cherry red cheeks.

"Mrs. Bing, these days women don't have to look a certain way or dress a certain way to please a man. He should be pleased with her company no matter what." Ally walked around the front of the counter and took her hair tie out to let her brown hair flow over her shoulders. "Now, I really do have to close up, or I'm going to be late, and that would be quite rude."

"Just consider putting your hair up in a nice style, darling." Mrs. Cale caught a tendril of it as she passed by, and gave it a light tug.

"Mrs. Cale!" Ally laughed as she batted her hand away. "I don't know what the three of you are up to, but I don't have time to find out. I'll stop at home and freshen up, okay? But I won't have time to do that if the three of you don't get going." She shooed them toward the door.

"Don't forget lipstick!" Mrs. Bing called out as Ally shut and locked the door.

Ally rolled her eyes as she flipped the open sign to closed. When she turned to walk away, she caught sight of her reflection in the glass doors.

Maybe they were right. She could clean up a bit, considering the smudges of chocolate on her pants, and the sheen of sweat on her skin. Luke never seemed to care about how she looked, but she hadn't put much effort in lately, and he had seemed quite distracted. They had both been so busy that they rarely had time to spend together.

The last time she spoke to him on the phone he confirmed their date for that night, then rushed her off as if he had something better to do. It wasn't like him, but she assumed it had to do with the cases he was investigating.

Ally went through the closing routine, then headed back to the cottage she once shared with her grandmother. Charlotte Sweet had moved to Freely Lakes, a retirement village that she loved. But Ally still missed coming home to her. When she opened the door, she was greeted by the shrill squeal of a pig, and the pitter-patter of cat paws.

"Arnold, Peaches!" Ally smiled as she crouched down to greet them. "At least you two don't care if I am covered in chocolate, hm?"

Arnold sniffed the leg of her pants, then tried to lick some of the chocolate from her knee.

"Arnold!" Ally laughed as she gave the pot-bellied pig a gentle push away.

Peaches purred as Ally stroked her fur.

"Okay, I've got to get you two fed and get changed, since now I have chocolate and pig drool on my pants." Ally rolled her eyes. After she'd fed them, she hurried to her bedroom to change.

Again, thoughts about Luke's absences lately crept into her mind. They had been together for quite some time, was he losing interest? Mrs. Bing, Mrs. Cale, and Mrs. White always knew what was going on around town. Had they heard a rumor about Luke being bored with her?

The thought made Ally's stomach twist. She rolled her eyes at her own reflection as she smoothed down the skirt of a beautiful, summer dress she had put on. Luke was the most trustworthy man she'd ever met. He'd never been anything but kind to her, and she doubted that he would string her along if he wasn't interested.

Still, as Ally smoothed her hair back from her face, a faint flutter in her heartbeat caused her to feel a little dizzy. What if?

Ally pushed the thoughts from her mind and grabbed her purse and keys. She blew kisses to Arnold and Peaches on her way out the door, then hurried to her car.

Luke had asked her to meet him at the

restaurant. Why hadn't he offered to pick her up? Her heart pounded as she started the engine. What if he didn't think they would be leaving together? She bit into her bottom lip and steered the car in the direction of the restaurant.

By The Pond was a new restaurant and the fanciest in Blue River. It showcased local produce from Blue River and the surrounding towns. Luckily, the drive wasn't long enough for her to talk herself into complete paranoia, but by the time she walked through the door of the restaurant, her nerves were on edge. She spotted Luke at a table in the back corner and smiled as she waved to him.

Luke waved to her, but his smile was thin and weak.

Ally glanced at the time on her phone to be sure she wasn't late. A minute or two. Would that really bother him? She doubted it.

"Hi sweetheart." Ally leaned down to kiss him in the same moment that he stood up to greet her. Her lips slammed into his forehead at an awkward angle that caused a burst of pain. "Ouch!"

"I'm so sorry." Luke sank back down into his chair and grabbed for his napkin. "Are you bleeding?" As he picked up the napkin, all of the silverware it contained spilled out and clattered to the floor.

"I'm okay, really." Ally reached down to pick up the silverware in the same moment that he did and knocked her head into his.

"Ouch!" Luke winced as he leaned back and touched his head.

"Oh no!" Ally couldn't help but laugh as she kissed the side of his head. "I'm so sorry. Look at us, we're a mess." She grinned as she held the silverware out to him.

"No." Luke cupped her cheek as he gazed into her eyes. "You're not a mess. You are stunning."

"Luke." Ally rolled her eyes and pulled away from him. As she settled in the chair across from him, she did her best to ignore the slight burn in her lips. How much more awkward could they be?

"Here you are, sir." A young waiter delivered a fresh set of silverware to Luke. "I trust all else is well?" Ally recognized him from around town.

"Yes Lester, thank you." Luke gave him a brief smile.

Lester glanced over at Ally.

"May I get you a glass of wine?"

"Sure, thanks." Ally tipped her head toward Luke. "Whatever he's having is fine."

"Oh actually, I'm just having cider." Luke cleared his throat.

"Really?" Ally raised an eyebrow. She knew that Luke enjoyed wine with dinner when they went out and he wasn't on call, which was a rare occurrence. "Sure, that sounds good to me." As the waiter walked away, Ally reached across the table and took Luke's hand. "Are you okay? I'm sorry that I was a little late."

"Nothing to apologize for." Luke looked into her eyes. "Ally, I want this night to be special."

"It is." Ally smiled and gave his hand a light squeeze. "I'm here with you."

"Ally, when we first met, you took my breath away—"

"What are those three doing?" Ally frowned as she looked out the window at Mrs. Bing, Mrs. Cale, and Mrs. White. The three women practically had their noses pressed against the glass.

"Ally?" Luke frowned as he drew his hand back from hers.

"I'm so sorry, Luke, you were saying?" Ally looked back at him, and watched as he fumbled in his pocket.

"We've had such a wonderful time together." Luke met her eyes.

Ally's heart pounded. Was this it? Had he invited her out to a special dinner just to suggest that they part ways?

"Luke, I've loved spending time with you." Ally searched his eyes for any hint of what his intentions might be.

"Your cider." The young waiter returned with two glasses on a small tray. "Would you like to order now?" He placed the glasses down on the table.

"No!" Luke shifted in his chair and shot an annoyed look in the waiter's direction. "Please, give us a few minutes."

"Certainly." The waiter backed away.

Ally looked back at Luke.

"Are you okay? You seem out of sorts. Maybe we should just eat in tonight." Ally started to stand up from the table.

"Ally, no." Luke caught her hand, then started to stand up. Before he could he fell to the ground, stopping himself when his knee hit the floor.

Ally thought he must have tripped over the long tablecloth, but before she could ask if he was okay, she heard several ear-piercing screams from outside the restaurant.

"What was that?" Ally pulled her hand free of Luke's and ran for the door.

Luke was right on her heels.

"What is it?" Luke pushed past her, and the rest of the crowd that had gathered around the edge of the pond that gave the restaurant its name, By The Pond. She noticed Mrs. Bing, Mrs. White, and Mrs. Cale all gathered together and clinging to one another. When she looked past them, she saw the outstretched arms of a man sprawled across the grass near the edge of the pond. Another man knelt beside him, his clothes soaked from head to toe.

"I saw him in the water," the man stammered. As he stood up, Luke ran over to him. "I thought I could help. I pulled him out." He shivered. "He's dead."

A mixture of screams and gasps, followed by whispers carried through the crowd of customers that had all poured out of the restaurant.

Ally noticed the waiter who had served her. He froze near the edge of the crowd, then took off at a run. As she turned her attention back to Luke, she watched him switch into detective mode. He whipped a tissue out of his pocket and picked up a piece of a broken wine bottle. The remnants were scattered across the grass beside the body.

"Everyone, stand back." Luke stood up and held

his hands up in the air. One hand held his badge for everyone to see. "Please back away from the scene."

Ally knew what his serious expression meant. This was no accident. The man that had been pulled out of the pond, had been murdered!

CHAPTER 2

Ally shuddered at the thought that the man had been killed. As she wrapped her arms around herself, she felt her sundress flutter in the light breeze. Gone were the thoughts about what she should wear, or why Luke was acting so strange. Now, her only focus was the body on the ground. Was he a local? Did she know him? It was hard to get a good look from the distance she was at.

Mrs. Cale, Mrs. White, and Mrs. Bing rushed over to her. "Oh, Ally it's so terrible!" Mrs. Bing's voice shook.

"Yes, it is." Ally frowned as she wrapped her arms around her. "I'm so sorry that you had to see this."

Ally recalled the strange way they watched her

through the window of the restaurant, but decided it was not the best time to ask about it.

"Did you know him?"

"He doesn't look familiar to me." Mrs. Bing shook her head.

"I haven't met him." Mrs. Cale tipped her head to the side. "He looks so young, maybe only in his forties, poor fellow. But the man who tried to save him, that man I know." She looked at the man that Luke led off to an uncrowded area, as police cars began to arrive. "That's Benson Dillow, he runs River Winery out on seventy-two."

"Oh, you're right, it is him." Mrs. Bing squinted at him. "I couldn't tell because the water smoothed down those curly, blond locks." She waved her hand in front of her. "So very handsome, and a hero. Who could ask for more?"

"Calm down, a man is dead." Mrs. White crossed her arms. "This is hardly the time to be hankering after a man who could be your grandson."

"Grandson?" Mrs. Bing coughed. "Not a chance. He has to be at least in his thirties, and I'm only in my early fifties." She batted her lashes.

"Plus twenty." Mrs. Cale nudged her with her elbow.

"Plus thirty." Mrs. White rolled her eyes.

Ally tuned out the conversation around her as she focused on Luke. She watched him walk back to the broken bottle. He crouched down and used a pen to lift a portion of the glass on the ground. He snapped a few pictures with his phone, then instructed one of the officers to collect the evidence.

Luke turned to survey the crowd, and his eyes met hers. She saw his serious expression shift into something that looked like disappointment to her. He lowered his head as he walked over to her.

"I'm sorry this night turned into a mess." He met her eyes.

"Don't be, it's not your fault." Ally stroked his cheek. "It looks pretty terrible. What are you thinking?"

"Not much right now." Luke sighed. "I need to get back into the restaurant and ask to see their wine collection." He glanced at the three ladies gathered close, nodded to them and offered a small smile, then steered Ally away from them. "So, about tonight."

"Don't worry about it, Luke. It was just dinner." Ally shrugged as she looked back at the crime scene. "Nothing is as important as this."

"Oh." Luke tried to meet her eyes. "Are you sure?"

"Yes, of course I'm sure. I'm not going to stop you from doing your job. You're the best detective, and whoever was killed deserves to have you on the case." Ally looked into his eyes. "I know you'll figure out what happened in no time."

"Thanks Ally." Luke's lips curved upward into a faint smile as he studied her, but it vanished the moment someone called his name. "I'd better get back to it." He fiddled in his pocket for a moment, then sighed as he turned to join the other officers.

Ally kept her eye on him. The moment he broke away from the other officers and headed for the restaurant, she followed after him. Ally knew that she would find out some information about the murder from the news and gossip. But she had a burning curiosity that wouldn't be satisfied with anything less than all of the information she could possibly get. She slipped back into the restaurant a few steps behind him.

"Ally?" Luke glanced over his shoulder at her with a furrowed brow.

"Just getting my purse." Ally pointed to the table they once occupied. Briefly she recalled him tripping over the tablecloth and smiled to herself.

A great detective, but a clumsy one. At least tonight.

"You'll be okay getting home?" Luke paused near the door of the kitchen.

"Sure, I will be." Ally nodded as she slipped her purse over her shoulder.

Luke stepped through the door of the kitchen, and she lingered for a moment. When she thought the coast would be clear, she crept up to the door and opened it just enough to hear the voices inside.

"Do you carry this kind of wine here?" Luke asked.

Ally peeked through the crack and watched as Luke held up his phone to the manager of the restaurant.

"We do." The manager smoothed his light brown hair back over his head, then wiped his hand down the length of his button-down shirt. "Why are you asking about it?"

"I believe a bottle of wine might have been used in the incident that just took place outside of this restaurant, and I would like to see the bottles that you have, along with any records of inventory and sales." Luke glanced up at the corners of the restaurant. "Do you have cameras in here? Out in the parking lot?"

"No, no cameras." The manager coughed, then gestured to a door at the back of the kitchen. "I can show you where the wine is."

Ally let the door close all the way just as Luke glanced in her direction. Her heart raced as she wondered if he had spotted her. She took a step back from the door and looked out through the front windows of the restaurant. The flashing lights and sirens had drawn the attention of those out in town for the night and residents who had wandered from their homes. In the sea of faces, she had to wonder if there might be a killer among them. A shiver crept up the length of her spine. She heard some commotion from inside the kitchen, and cracked the door open again.

"I don't understand how this could happen!" The manager's voice grew high-pitched and shaky. "I took inventory this morning before we opened. All of that wine was there. Now it's gone! There is no way we served so much. It must have been stolen!"

"I'm going to have a few officers conduct a search of the premises. In the meantime, I would like you to make me a list of everyone who would have had access to the wine between this morning and this moment. Can you do that please?" The sharpness in Luke's tone drifted through the open door.

Ally bit down into her bottom lip. She knew that voice. It meant that he suspected that the manager wasn't telling him the truth.

"Yes of course, you may search whatever you like. I should call the owner." The manager shook his head as he pulled his phone out of his pocket. "She's not going to be happy about it."

"Can you give me the name and contact information of the owner please?" Luke pulled out his notepad and pen.

"Sure. It's Cynthia Cooper, and she's going to be so upset." The manager sighed, then rattled off the phone number for Cynthia.

As Ally backed away from the door, she wondered who the victim might be. His face had been covered so quickly that she doubted that many people had the chance to get a good look at him. She stepped out of the restaurant, and directly into the path of her grandmother.

"Ally!" She gasped, then threw her arms around her.

"It's okay, Mee-Maw, I'm okay." Ally hugged her back, then looked into her eyes. "What are you doing here?"

"I was at home playing cards in the community room and one of the residents mentioned that something happened here. I tried calling and I couldn't get hold of you." Charlotte pressed her hand against her chest. "I knew that you were supposed to be here with Luke, and I just got so frightened that something might have happened to you." She cupped Ally's cheeks and stared straight into her eyes. "You're sure that you're okay?"

"Yes, I'm fine." Ally shook her head. "How did you know that Luke and I were going to be here tonight? I just mentioned we were having dinner, I didn't know where we were going until a couple of hours ago."

"Oh, there's Mrs. Bing." Charlotte waved to her friend.

"Charlotte." Mrs. Bing waved back. "Charlotte come quick, we're planning a vigil."

"A vigil?" Ally frowned. "But they don't even know who the victim is yet." She followed her grandmother over to the three women, who stood in a circle, each with a phone in their hands.

"I've already tweeted it." Mrs. White glanced up at the others.

"No, you didn't." Mrs. Cale huffed and held out her phone. "I tweeted it, you retweeted it."

"Stop arguing and just get the word out." Mrs. Bing frowned and shot a sharp look at each woman. "If you two keep it up no one will even show up."

"Mrs. Bing, how can you be planning a vigil?" Ally glanced in the direction of the medical examiner's van that pulled up to the scene. "They haven't even identified the body, yet."

"Maybe they haven't, but I have." Mrs. Bing tapped on her phone a few times then held up the phone for both Ally and Charlotte to see. "It's Mel Cambridge. He's a wine critic, a quite famous one." She quirked an eyebrow. "I couldn't be sure at first, but then I noticed his shoes. I would know those shoes anywhere. I met him a few days ago when I took a tour of Ballington Winery in Freely. He is quite an impressive man, and not just because of his shoes."

"Mrs. Bing, are you certain that it's him?" Ally looked toward the body and noticed the wing tipped shoes that stuck out from the sheet.

"Oh, I'm certain, as certain as I can be." Mrs. Bing nodded, then tapped the screen of her phone a few more times. "Wait until my wine-tasting group hears about this."

"Hold on!" Ally clapped her hands to get their full attention. "Listen ladies, I know you think you have a hunch about who the victim is, but none of you should be making it public knowledge until his identity has been confirmed and his family has been contacted. Just think how the family will feel if they discover their loved one's death on some social media post."

"She's right." Charlotte nodded as she looked at her friends. "We need to keep this to ourselves until we can learn more about what happened here."

"I know exactly what happened here." Mrs. White crossed her arms. "He obviously didn't like someone's wine."

"We don't know that for sure." Ally frowned as she watched Luke hurry across the space between the restaurant and the body. He looked in her direction briefly, then turned his attention to the medical examiner. "Any number of things could have led to his death."

"It could have, but he has rated many wines from this area and he was here to do a special on Ballington Winery for their two-hundred year anniversary." Mrs. Bing sighed and finally lowered her phone. "It's both a blessing and a curse to wineries when he rates their wines or visits the local places. His opinion is so valued that a good review from him could turn a nobody into a millionaire, but a bad review could go a long way to ruin a winery's reputation and their business, too."

"You seem to know a lot about him." Ally peered at Mrs. Bing. "Are you a big fan?"

"Not so much of him, but of his podcast. He holds competitions, and does specials and features on some wines and wineries. He records everything. It's fun to listen to. Benson sent one of his wines in to be reviewed about a month ago and Mel gave it a rave review." Mrs. Bing shrugged as she looked over at Mrs. White. "Let's just delete the tweet and put a hold on the vigil, and make sure his family is happy to have one. I'm sure his identity will be released soon enough."

"Good plan." Mrs. White sighed as she looked at the crowd gathered around the crime scene. "The vultures are going to have a field day with this. A famous name, killed in a small town."

"That will make Luke's job twice as hard." Ally frowned, then turned away from the group. "I'm going to see what I can find out about his visit to

Blue River. Maybe someone saw him in the area tonight."

"He was staying with his wife Jeanne, at Riverside." Mrs. Bing lowered her voice. "No one is supposed to know that, but you know I have my sources."

"Thanks Mrs. Bing." Ally looked in the direction of the new motel. "That's not far from here, I think I'll head over. I know the owner, maybe she can give me some information."

"I'll come with you." Charlotte followed after her.

"Mee-Maw, you don't have to do that, it's getting late." Ally looked over at her with a frown.

"Nonsense. Besides, I want to hear all about your dinner with Luke." Charlotte hooked her arm around Ally's.

"It didn't happen." Ally shrugged, then bit into her bottom lip. "Have you noticed him acting strangely lately, Mee-Maw?"

"Luke?" Charlotte raised an eyebrow. "Well, he does take his job a little too seriously, but other than that not really. Why?"

"No reason." Ally led the way toward the motel.

They reached the parking lot, when another piercing scream stopped them both in their tracks.

CHAPTER 3

$\mathcal{A}$lly took a sharp breath as she witnessed a woman fall to her knees in front of one of the motel room doors. A police officer leaned down to help her back to her feet.

"I'm very sorry for your loss," the officer murmured, but Ally heard him as she walked closer.

"That must be his wife. Jeanne," Charlotte whispered to Ally, as the woman leaned against the wall beside the door and grasped the officer's arm.

"There must be some mistake. He was just out for dinner. Just to help him relax and unwind. Are you sure it was him?" Her voice trembled as she spoke.

"I'm sure, ma'am, but we will need you to make

an official identification." The officer gestured to his patrol car. "Would you mind coming with me?"

"I can't believe this." Jeanne began to weep as the officer led her to the car. "My Mel! How could this have happened? He just walked off, and now he's gone?"

Ally watched as the door started to close behind the woman.

"Ally?" Charlotte gave her arm a light tug. "Look, the curtains are open, let's take a peek." She pointed to the windows of Jeanne's room as the patrol car pulled away. "You said you wanted to find out more about him, this might be our chance." She tipped her head toward the room. "Let's go have a look."

"Okay." Ally followed her grandmother toward the window.

"I'm sure the police will want to search in there." Charlotte tried to peer through the window.

"Charlotte?" A female voice called out from behind them.

"Sandy." Charlotte turned to face the woman. "It's good to see you."

"You too. What are you doing here?" Sandy's smile grew wider. "Are you two already trying to solve Mel's murder?" Sandy was a regular at

Charlotte's Chocolate Heaven. She was in her fifties and a Blue River local. She had recently opened the Riverside Motel.

"You know us too well. But how do you know about Mel?" Charlotte narrowed her eyes.

"The police just told me." Sandy shook her head. "It's just terrible."

"It is." Charlotte tried to hide the fact that she was a bit startled because they had been caught snooping, but she decided to see if she could use it to her advantage. "Luke won't be able to search the place until he gets a warrant. Can you tell us anything that might help?"

"Not much." Sandy shrugged. "Mel and Jeanne booked the room for the week. They were due to leave in three days." She shook her head. "Neither of them could have expected something like this."

"Maybe not." Ally nodded. "But I wonder, if his reputation was so good that he could ruin peoples' livelihoods and their lives when he didn't like a glass of wine, how many enemies has he made over the length of his career?"

"That's a good question," Charlotte agreed.

"I'm sure Luke will find out about any threats he might have received." Ally nodded to Sandy. "Anything else? Did he act odd?"

"No, not really." Sandy smiled then looked thoughtful. "There was one incident when he couldn't find the key to his briefcase in his pocket. He had a locked briefcase with him and carried it most places. I heard him shout at Jeanne that he couldn't find the key. But then he found it. But that's all I heard from them really."

"Thanks Sandy." Charlotte started to turn away. "See you in the chocolate shop soon?"

"Yes, of course." Sandy walked off as Ally and Charlotte walked around the back to head toward their cars. As they did, they passed the back porch of Mel and Jeanne's room. There was a skirt and blouse hung over a chair on the porch. Small droplets of water gathered on the floor.

"This is a bit odd." Ally stopped and placed her hands on her hips. "Why would her clothes be soaking wet?"

"Maybe she washed them in the tub and is drying them outside." Charlotte glanced over at the clothes. "It's easier than hitting the laundromat sometimes."

"I guess."

"We should get home." Charlotte and Ally took two steps and noticed Luke walking toward them.

"Ally." Luke met her eyes, then looked over at

Charlotte. "Charlotte. What are you two doing here?"

"We just went for a walk." Ally shrugged. "We thought maybe we could find out more about Mel and his wife."

"Really?" Luke crossed his arms. "There was no part of you that thought that might be a bad idea?"

"We just spoke to Sandy." Charlotte smiled at him. "No harm done."

"You can't know that." Luke narrowed his eyes.

"Relax Luke." Ally took a deep breath as his eyes searched hers. "We spoke to Sandy. Apparently Mel had a briefcase. Do you know if he had it with him?"

"You need to go home and stay out of this." Luke pointed toward the parking lot.

"Luke." Ally moved closer to him and reached for his arm.

"I mean it." Luke stared into her eyes. "This murder is going to turn a spotlight on Blue River, the entire police department, and especially me. I can't risk having anything going wrong."

"Okay. I'm sorry." Ally locked her eyes to his.

"I'll speak to you later." Luke turned and walked away from them.

Ally's heart sank as she followed after her

grandmother. After their awkward dinner, the last thing she wanted to do was increase the tension between them. But there wasn't much she could do to change that now.

"Are you okay, Ally?" Charlotte wrapped her arm around Ally's waist.

"I'm fine. Maybe we shouldn't have come here." Ally sighed.

"Luke may be a great detective, but you and I know this town and the residents better than he ever could. Most of them talk to us freely. It doesn't hurt to have a look, ask some questions and help him if we can." Charlotte steered her back toward the restaurant. "It's been a long night, maybe we should start fresh in the morning."

"You're right. That's a good idea. I'd like to go to Benson's winery tomorrow if it's open. He's the one who found Mel. I bet he has some information that he could share with us." Ally paused in the parking lot of the restaurant.

"You're not worried about stepping on Luke's toes?" Charlotte met her eyes.

"I'll be careful." Ally smiled. "He does have delicate feet."

"Seriously, Ally." Charlotte draped her arm

around her shoulders. "He is right about there being a spotlight on this investigation."

"And on him." Ally glanced back in the direction of the motel. "Which means he'll need my support more than ever." She looked at her grandmother again. "Tomorrow afternoon? Since the shop is closed, I can make the chocolates in the morning and then we can spend as much time as we need to at the winery."

"Perfect. I'll meet you at the shop in the morning, then we can go to Benson's for around two? We can go home and feed the pets and then be on our way."

"Great." Ally smiled. "Do you need a lift home?"

"No thanks, I've got Jeff's car." Charlotte pointed toward the car. "I'll see you in the morning." She stepped back from her granddaughter and looked her over. "No investigating without me."

"I'm going straight home." Ally held up her hands and smiled. "I promise."

"Good." Charlotte walked off down the sidewalk toward Jeff's car.

Ally opened the door to her car, then took a breath. When she'd gotten into the car earlier that night, she'd been nervous about her date with Luke. Now, she wondered if she had just given him more reason to want to end their relationship. Her grandmother was right, she needed to be extra careful, but not just because of the spotlight on the case. Luke had something weighing on his mind, she had no doubt about that. If it was about her, she didn't want him to decide he'd had enough. Her chest tightened at the thought. She started the car, and looked out through the windshield at the busy street ahead of her, full of the residents of Blue River, who no longer felt safe. No matter what was at risk, she had to try help solve the murder, she couldn't just sit around and do nothing.

CHAPTER 4

The buzz of Ally's phone drew her from a deep sleep. She reached for it, and nearly knocked it off her bedside table. As she turned it over in her hand, she saw a text from Luke. She also saw a notice that she had missed her alarm. She was late to meet her grandmother at the shop.

"Oh no!" Ally sighed as she sat up and skimmed the text from Luke.

I'm sorry if I was harsh yesterday. Just checking in. I hope we can reschedule dinner soon.

As Ally was about to reply, her phone rang. She answered straight away.

"I'm at the shop, where are you?" Charlotte's cheerful voice was on the other end.

"Sorry, I overslept. I just woke up. Somehow, I didn't hear my alarm go off. I'll be there soon."

"Okay, I'll get started." Charlotte laughed.

After a quick shower, Ally dressed, then headed into the kitchen, followed by two hungry animals.

"I know, I know, breakfast is late." Ally rolled her eyes as she filled their dishes. "I must have been more tired than I realized." She set their bowls down on the floor, then gave each one a light pet.

"Peaches, make sure you don't eat all of that in one bite." Ally put her hands on her hips and laughed. "Who would expect the pig to be the polite eater?"

Arnold gave a short snort.

"No offense, Arnold." Ally smiled at him.

After Ally and Charlotte spent the morning making chocolates, Charlotte dropped Ally off at the cottage then went to Freely Lakes to get ready for their visit to the winery.

Ally made sure the animals had everything they needed for the afternoon and let them out the back to have a play around. She watched them and giggled as Arnold chased Peaches around in circles.

As soon as Arnold and Peaches had come inside, Ally heard the front door open.

"I'm here, Ally!" Charlotte walked into the

kitchen dressed in a sleek, black pants suit, set off with a large, silver pin near her left shoulder.

"Mee-Maw." Ally hugged her grandmother. "I see you've dressed the part."

"Do as others do." Charlotte winked at Ally. "Jeans again, hm?"

"Why does everyone keep asking me that?" Ally looked down at her jeans. "They're clean."

"That's a start." Charlotte grinned as she looked through the window at the clear, blue sky. "It's a perfect day for heading out into the countryside." She smiled as she reached down to pet Arnold. "You know the website says the winery is animal friendly. Maybe we should bring our best pals along."

"Remember, Mee-Maw, we're just going there to have a look around and ask some questions to see if we can try to find out more about the murder." Ally slung her purse over her shoulder.

"Maybe, but that doesn't mean that we can't enjoy the afternoon as well." Charlotte shrugged.

"That's true." Ally rolled her eyes as Peaches rubbed against her leg. "It looks like someone definitely wants to come along." She scooped the cat up. "Alright, we can make an afternoon adventure out of it. I just hope that we're able to find some kind of information about Mel's murder."

"Alright, Arnold, let's go." Charlotte opened the front door and the pot-bellied pig bolted for the car.

"I guess he's ready to go." Ally laughed and carried Peaches to the car. Once the animals were settled in the back seat, Ally got in the front.

"So, you and Luke didn't even get the chance to talk at dinner last night?" Charlotte glanced over at her.

"Not really. It was strange, we kept bumping into each other, and then he actually tripped over the tablecloth." Ally laughed, then shook her head. "I guess it just wasn't meant to be last night. Then after that he caught us near Mel's room." She groaned. "He seemed upset. But he texted me this morning. Oh no." She sighed. "I forgot to text him back."

"I'm sorry that your date got ruined for you. I'm sure you were looking forward to it." Charlotte pointed out the turn she should take.

"It was just dinner, nothing too exciting really." Ally turned down the street, then sped up a bit. "It should only take us about forty minutes to get there."

"I'm surprised I've never been there before, with it being quite close by." Charlotte squinted at her phone. "The winery has been around for years, but it looks like it only opened last year to the public. I suppose word hasn't gotten around about it."

"According to Mrs. Bing, Mel had recently given Benson a rave review for the wine he sent in for judging so I guess word had certainly started to travel. He's a renowned wine critic. His opinion of wine is famous around the world. He reviews wines for Sip, Eat and Savor, a gourmet food and wine magazine, and visits some of the wineries and restaurants as well." Ally turned down another road, then glanced at the pets in the rearview mirror. "These two do love their car rides, don't they?"

"Like two peas in a pod." Charlotte smiled at Peaches nestled up against Arnold's side. "I do miss having them around my feet all the time."

"They miss you, too." Ally leaned over some as she looked at her grandmother. "I do, too. But we're all happy you've found a great place and you're so happy there."

"I do like it at Freely Lakes. They plan so many activities. Of course, I have to drag Jeff to all of them." Charlotte laughed. "I'm not sure that he appreciates that."

"He seems to appreciate anytime he gets with you." Ally navigated around a slow car. "I think it's sweet."

"It is sweet." Charlotte smiled as she sat back against her seat. "I really like having Jeff's companionship. When you and Luke first started dating, I really liked the way he treated you, and now I'm surprised to find that Jeff treats me in a very similar way."

"Yes, things were so nice back then." Ally swallowed hard as she tried to push away troubling thoughts. They had spent so much time together in the beginning. But he had been busy with work, and ever since she had taken over the chocolate shop, she had been extra busy, too. Was that what the dinner was about? Him deciding it was time for them to part ways? After the way he talked to her last night, she wondered if he'd just had enough of her.

"They're still nice now, aren't they?"

"Of course they are. It's just we don't get much time together, and sometimes I get caught up in the routine and pressure of the shop, and I forget to make an extra effort to be available to him when he's free. We couldn't even pull off dinner last night." Ally shook her head. "I just worry sometimes."

"Worry about what?" Charlotte pointed to the

street ahead of them. "After we turn here, it's about five minutes up the road."

"Okay, great." Ally turned down the road.

"Ally?" Charlotte looked over at her. "What are you worried about?"

"Nothing. It's silly." Ally took a sharp breath at the sight of the towering trees that lined the road. "It is gorgeous here. What a hidden gem!"

"It doesn't look too busy, there are only a few cars in the parking lot." Charlotte gathered her purse. "I'm sure we'll have plenty of time to explore."

"I'm glad I brought Peaches' leash." Ally stepped out of the car. "She could roam forever here."

"Oh, I'm sure she's going to love that." Charlotte grinned.

Peaches stared at Ally as she held up the leash.

"It's for your safety, love." Ally met her eyes, then crouched down and attempted to attach the leash to Peaches' harness.

The cat gave a loud yowl and swatted at Ally's hand.

"Yikes!" Charlotte grinned. "She's not too happy."

"At least she kept her claws in." Ally rolled her eyes, then managed to secure the leash. "I don't know why she doesn't like the harness anymore. I think she wants complete freedom now."

Peaches slunk out of the car with her head down.

"Oh, don't pout, we're going to have a nice time." Ally gave her a light pet, then headed in the direction of a large, white building. Before they could reach the door, a man greeted them.

"Hello and welcome to River Winery." He smiled as he offered his hand. "My name is Benson Dillow, I'm the owner of this winery."

"It's a pleasure to meet you." Ally shook his hand, and locked her eyes to his. She recognized him from the night before as the man that had tried to help Mel. She also recalled Mrs. Bing's description of his good looks, and she had to admit, as his blond curls ruffled in the light wind, she wasn't wrong. "I'm Ally Sweet, and this is my grandmother, Charlotte Sweet."

Arnold gave a loud snort, and nudged Benson's leg.

Ally laughed and tugged Arnold back.

"And this is Arnold, sorry, he's very friendly."

"Aren't you an interesting creature?" Benson gazed down at him. "We've had dogs visit since we opened to the public, and even a goat, but never a pig." He offered his hand to Charlotte. "It's nice to meet you."

"Nice to meet you as well." Charlotte gave his hand a firm shake. "We also have Peaches with us today." She pointed out the cat who sprawled out in the grass in a patch of sunlight. "I hope you don't mind us dropping in like this. Your website did say animal friendly."

"That's right, everyone is welcome. We're not very busy today. We do however have a tasting tour starting in about twenty minutes if you'd be interested in joining it." Benson glanced over his shoulder toward the building. "We only have a handful of people signed up for it."

"That surprises me." Ally narrowed her eyes. "It's such a beautiful day."

"Yes, it is. But Ballington Winery is having a special anniversary sale, and since they've been in operation in the area a lot longer than I have, I suppose that winery is more popular." Benson winced. "I hope I haven't just convinced you to go there instead."

"No, we're here to check this place out." Ally glanced around. "What made you decide to buy a winery in Mainbry?"

"Actually, it chose me in a way. I inherited a

share of the winery and vineyard from a great-uncle of mine. When the other owner passed away, I managed to buy the rest of it. You could say the opportunity showed up at the right time in my life. I was ready for a change after my divorce, now here I am." Benson smiled at them both.

"Ally's divorced, too." Charlotte gazed down a path that wound around the side of the building. "Does that lead to the vines?"

"Mee-Maw." Ally sighed and gave her a light nudge with her elbow. Her grandmother was always so open with people, which often left Ally embarrassed. She preferred to keep to herself and leave the past in the past.

"Oh?" Benson met her eyes. "It's not an easy thing, is it?"

"It was some time ago for me." Ally forced a smile. "But no, it's never easy."

"Ally! Charlotte! Hello!" A loud voice bellowed from the parking lot.

Ally turned to see Mrs. Bing, Mrs. Cale, and Mrs. White, headed in their direction.

"Excuse me, ladies." Benson nodded to both of them. "I'm going to get things set up for the next tour, I do hope you'll join in."

"We'll be there." Ally nodded in return as Charlotte walked over to greet her friends.

"I didn't know you two planned to be here today." Mrs. Bing hugged Ally as she walked over.

"We didn't." Ally greeted Mrs. Cale, and Mrs. White as well. "We decided to have a look around. What about you three?"

"Well, I had been meaning to get out here." Mrs. White glanced around at the lush grass and towering trees. "A little nature always soothes the soul."

"We could all use some soul soothing after what happened last night." Mrs. Cale shook her head. "We wanted to show our support for Benson, too. At least he tried to save Mel."

"He seems like a kind man. I think he would like us to have a look around." Charlotte looked toward the door he'd walked through. "There's a tour starting shortly, do you want to join us?"

"That would be wonderful." Mrs. White nodded. "A little wine tasting never did any harm." She winked at Ally.

"I won't have any wine so I can drive back." Charlotte looked toward Ally.

"You don't have to do that, Mee-Maw. I don't need to taste the wine." Ally shook her head.

"I don't mind." Charlotte smiled. "You can have a few sips, I don't feel like any at the moment anyway."

"Thanks Mee-Maw."

Charlotte walked faster to catch up to Mrs. Bing and Mrs. Cale.

As the others walked ahead of them, Mrs. White linked her arm around Ally's.

"So, I hear dinner was canceled last night?"

"It had to be." Ally nodded as she looked over at Mrs. White. Her silver curls lightly grazed the skin of her cheeks, and her long, dark lashes framed her clear blue eyes with such sharp contrast that they seemed an unnatural shade. Ally could recall many times that Mrs. White had pulled her aside for a heart-to-heart when she was a child. She always told Ally like it was, never sugarcoated anything, or treated her like a child. "It seems we have a hard time getting together lately."

"Life can be that way." Mrs. White nodded, and gave her arm a light pat as they continued through the door of the building. "The important thing is to never let life stop you from having the time you need."

"That is very good advice, Mrs. White, thank you." Ally smiled at her as she tightened Peaches' leash to prevent her from investigating the shoes of the others gathered near the front desk.

"Don't thank me, just act on it." Mrs. White met her eyes. "So many years slip by without us ever noticing."

Ally noted the hint of sadness in her voice. She slipped her arm around Mrs. White's waist and gave her a soft squeeze.

"I'm glad you're here with us today."

"Me too." Mrs. White smiled.

"I'm ready for some wine tasting! What's the hold up?" Mrs. Bing stared straight at Benson as he stood in front of the group.

"Welcome everyone." Benson smiled at Mrs. Bing, then the others. "Hannah will lead your tour today, but I'm going to tag along, too. If you have any questions along the way, please feel free to ask."

As Hannah led them through a rear door and down a wide path, Ally drank in the sight of the manicured gardens on either side of the dirt path. Instantly, she thought of sharing the experience with Luke. She was sure that it was something he would enjoy. She reached into her pocket and pulled out her phone. As she pulled up his last text, she thought about Mrs. White's words. Already that morning she'd forgotten to text him back a few times. If she wanted to see their relationship strengthen, she had to find a way to make him a priority.

Ally typed out a quick text back to him and hit send.

"Are we boring you?"

Ally looked up from her phone and into Benson's eyes.

"Oh sorry." She blushed as she dropped her phone into her purse. "Just a message I forgot to send."

"Oh, don't worry, I find these things a bit boring myself. I've heard the story so many times." Benson rubbed the back of his neck as he smiled. "My mind wanders."

"I seem to be having that problem a lot lately." Ally smiled.

"I have something that I think you might like." Benson's eyes shone as he looked into hers. "Would you mind breaking away from the group for just a few minutes?"

"Not at all." Ally glanced over at her grandmother who had a glass of water in her hand. Mrs. Cale, Mrs. White, and Mrs. Bing all had small, empty glasses of wine. "Give me just a moment." She stepped up to her grandmother. "Would you mind keeping track of Peaches? I'm just going to check something out with Benson."

"Sure, of course." Charlotte took Peaches' leash. "Did you want to taste the wine first?"

"No thanks. I don't want to keep Benson waiting." Ally started to turn away from the four women.

"Benson, huh?" Mrs. Bing looked past her at the man who waited at the edge of the group. "Does he know about your police detective boyfriend?" She spoke louder than she needed to.

"Mrs. Bing!" Ally narrowed her eyes. "That's quite enough. How much wine have you had?"

"Just one." Mrs. Bing held up her glass.

"And mine." Mrs. White raised an eyebrow.

"And mine." Mrs. Cale winced. "I wasn't ready for wine, yet."

"Don't worry, Ally, we'll keep a close eye on her." Charlotte gave Mrs. Bing a light pat on the back. "Let's go, there's more wine to taste."

"More wine?" Mrs. Bing perked up. "Show me the way."

Ally shook her head as she turned and walked back over to Benson.

"I'm sorry about that, they can act a little silly."

"A police detective boyfriend, hm?" Benson grinned. "I'll be sure to remember that."

"Where to?" Ally smiled.

"Just this way." Benson led her back toward the building.

Ally glanced over her shoulder in the direction of the group, then followed after him.

enson directed Ally to a door not far from the door that they had exited through for the tour.

"We have a storage cellar downstairs, I have a few of my favorite wines there. I'd love for you to try a sample." Benson glanced back at her as he flicked on a light switch that revealed stairs. "I have to admit something."

"What's that?" Ally followed behind him down the stairs.

"I might have had an idea of who you were before you introduced yourself." Benson reached the bottom of the stairs, then stepped aside to let her pass. "I've been looking into your shop for some time."

"You have?" The cooler temperature in the cellar caused goosebumps to scatter across her arms. "Why is that?"

"Your delicious candy, of course." Benson tipped his head from side to side and took a deep breath. "But I have also been concocting a plan. I'd like to purchase some of your chocolates to make gift boxes with some of my dessert wines. I'm just not sure which wines would complement which chocolates." He held up his hands. "I'm a bit hopeless when it comes to that. Forgive me for stealing you away from the tour, but I didn't want to pass up the opportunity for you to sample some of the wines and get your honest opinion." He walked down a narrow hallway. "When we have people who may want to make several purchases, we offer a free locked wine cabinet for them to keep their wine here on the property. It has the right conditions to preserve the wines and it's easier and cheaper than installing and maintaining your own wine cellar."

"Interesting, I'd never even thought of that." Ally paused as he opened another door. "I have to admit something too, Benson."

"You do?" Benson turned to face her.

"I didn't come here just to see your winery, though it's quite beautiful. I saw you try to help Mel last night, and I wanted to learn more about you." Ally shrugged. "I figured checking out your business would be the best way to do it. Did you know Mel well?"

"Not very well, I only met him briefly a few days ago when he visited the winery. But I think everyone who has ever bottled wine knows of Mel." Benson sighed, then shook his head. "I did try to help him, but I wasn't quick enough. I've been dodging calls from reporters all morning." He met her eyes. "You don't double as a journalist do you, Ally?"

"No, I don't." Ally smiled. "And I don't mean to be nosy, or to bring up a difficult topic. I'm sorry for that." She turned back toward the stairs. "Maybe I should go back."

"No wait." Benson smiled as she looked back at him. "It's alright. I don't mind if you have questions. I have a lot of questions of my own about what happened last night. Do you still want to try the wines?"

"I'd love to." Ally held his gaze.

"Right this way." Benson led her through the door which opened up into a square room, with banks of cabinets on all sides.

"Did Mel have a wine cabinet?" Ally swept her

gaze along the glass doors that housed each bank of cabinets.

"Actually, yes he did. When he toured the winery, he got one for while he was in town and filled it up." Benson sighed as he stepped farther into the room. "I suppose his wife will want to take possession of the wines now. What a tragedy." He glanced back at Ally. "It's always unsettling to think that a life can be cut short so easily. We take so much for granted."

"That's true." Ally followed him as he led the way down a short hallway. "So, Mel liked your wine?"

"Yes. He loved it. I sent my wine in when he was doing a judging panel a few weeks ago and he wrote an amazing review." Benson chuckled as he shoved his hands into his pockets. "He was highly regarded as a wine critic and his review did wonders for my winery."

"I've heard he was a very impressive man."

Benson continued down to the door on the other side of the room.

"This is one of the rooms where we have the wine storage cabinets, we have another one downstairs where the rest of the wines are stored."

He pulled open the door and revealed another set of stairs. "Last one, I promise."

"From the outside of the building, I never would have guessed that this place was so big. Do you have a lot of employees here?" Ally watched him descend the stairs in front of her.

"A few. I have four tour guides who also handle most of my customer service and a couple of them also work in the vineyard. There are also a few more that work in the vineyard seasonally, and a couple that maintain the building and the grounds. Here we are." Benson paused in front of a large space with a sealed glass door. "It's chilly inside, I'll bring some wines out for you to taste."

"Please." Ally shivered as she rubbed her arms. The lower level felt at least ten degrees cooler than the one above.

"Here." Benson shrugged off his blazer and offered it to her.

"Oh no, I'm fine, it's okay." Ally waved her hand.

"I insist." Benson draped his blazer across her shoulders.

"Thanks."

"I'll be right back with the wines." Benson opened the door to the sealed room.

Ally felt a cool wind carry through the door before he closed it. She tightened the blazer around her, grateful to have it.

"I brought out two for you to try." Benson lined the two bottles side by side on a small table outside of the sealed room. "They are my sweet wines. Late harvest and ice wine. This is my specialty." He picked up the last bottle. "Ice wine." He looked up at her and smiled. "The grapes have to be frozen on the vine before they are picked. It sounds simple but it's actually difficult to get the right conditions. But the results are delicious." He grabbed a glass from underneath the table and placed it on the table. As he poured Ally a glass, she noticed the rich yellow color of the wine.

"It looks delicious."

"Smell it." Benson held the glass up beneath her nose. "I'm serious." He grinned. "Trust me."

Ally took a sniff of the wine. Her eyes widened.

"Wow, it smells so sweet!"

"It does." Benson nodded. "Now, taste."

Ally reached for the glass and took the delicate stem from his grasp. She raised the glass to her lips and took a sip. The sweet flavor tickled across her tongue.

"It's delicious!" Ally nodded, then took a bigger

sip. "Oh, I'm definitely going to have to buy some of this."

"No need to buy it." Benson grabbed another bottle from inside the room and offered it to her. "Consider it a gift."

"That's so kind of you." Ally met his eyes. "I feel like I should be the one offering you things, since you're the hero."

"Hero?" Benson raised an eyebrow. "I don't think it counts if the person doesn't survive."

"You tried, that's what counts." Ally shifted the bottle from one hand to the other. "Not everyone would jump in to try to help."

"I guess it's second nature to keep an eye out for people in trouble." Benson frowned as he opened the other bottle and poured another small glass. "Please, try the late harvest, too."

"Thank you." Ally took the glass from him. "You have a talent for this." She took a sip of the wine, then closed her eyes. "Yes, this is just as good."

"I do enjoy dabbling with different blends." Benson shrugged. "I'll start you a wine cabinet, you should take a bottle of each of the wines with you, my treat. I'd love to hear what you think about which candies will pair well with them." He ducked back into the sealed room and grabbed another bottle of wine.

"I can see why Mel gave you such a great review." Ally smiled. "The wines are fantastic."

"Thank you, but he actually didn't taste these wines." Benson grimaced slightly. "He was only accepting dry red wines for judging at the time so I sent in my red blend."

"Well, these are delicious. Do you think I could see Mel's cabinet? I'm just curious about what wines he purchased. Maybe I will want to buy some of the same wines." Ally set down her wine glass. "Although, I'm not sure anything could beat the flavor of this wine."

"I'm so glad that you enjoyed it. I don't mind. I'm sure the police will want to see it soon enough." Benson tipped his head toward the room right across from them. "The cabinets are right over there."

"Does this place ever end?" Ally laughed as she followed behind him.

"I think it was built to survive a zombie apocalypse." Benson flashed a grin over his shoulder.

"Good to know." Ally continued into the room.

"We can set you up with one of the cabinets in

here as well. This is his cabinet." Benson's voice trailed off as he stared at the wide open glass door, and the empty space beyond it. "What's happened here?" He took a step back.

"What's wrong?" Ally looked past him at the wine cabinet. It was empty. "Did someone break in?"

"I think someone must have." Benson covered his mouth with his hand as his eyes widened. "I've never had anything like this happen before. I should call the police." He pulled out his phone, then tucked it back into his pocket. "Wait, maybe one of my employees knows something about this."

Benson pressed a button on the wall and spoke into a speaker. "All staff please report to the storage cabinets." He sighed as he turned back to Ally. "I'm sorry about all of this, but I'm going to need to question my staff."

"It's fine, I understand." Ally took a step back. "You really should call the police, though. If someone stole all of Mel's wine, then it could be the same person who is responsible for his death."

"I'm hoping that it's just some kind of mistake." Benson frowned.

"Maybe his wife already came and emptied out the cabinet?" Ally raised an eyebrow.

"Maybe. But we have some strict rules about who can access the cabinet, and as I recall Mel did not add his wife as a permitted visitor. Someone should have told me if she came to collect his wines." Benson looked toward the stairs as three people descended them. The first was a young woman about Ally's age, the second was a man of about the same age, and the third was a man who appeared to be in his fifties.

"Hannah is still running a tour." The woman frowned as she looked between Benson and Ally. "What is this all about?"

"Does anyone know what happened to Mel's wine?" Benson gestured to the empty cabinet behind him. "Who unlocked it?"

"I don't know anything about that." She shook her head and took a step back.

"Conner?" Benson locked his eyes to the young man. "Was it you?"

"What? No way." Conner shook his head. "I didn't want anything to do with that guy. He was so intimidating." He held up his hands.

"Mitchell?" Benson took a step toward him. "Did you unlock it?"

"Of course not." Mitchell narrowed his eyes. "I

would never do something like that without your permission."

"Well, someone did." Benson crossed his arms as he stared at the three.

"Maybe Alicia." Conner looked at the floor. "She has the day off but I'm sure she would have told you if Mel accessed his wine cabinet."

"Try and contact her for me." Benson demanded.

"Okay." Conner scurried away.

"Don't you have cameras?" Ally looked up into the corners of the room.

"No, many of our clients prefer their privacy, even if it sacrifices some aspects of security." Benson gestured to the stairs. "Maybe you should head up, I need to speak to these three a bit more."

"No one should look inside the cabinet." Ally stepped in front of the door and held up her hands. "Not until the police have a chance to investigate it."

"I won't cause any harm." Benson shrugged, then settled his gaze on her. "Please, this is private business."

"It's not, I'm sorry." Ally frowned as she noticed the tension in his expression. "This is part of a murder investigation, and the scene mustn't be contaminated."

"We don't know that." Benson stepped closer to

her. "Until I report it to the police, they don't know that either. You seem awfully invested in all of this."

"I know that considering the circumstances the police will want to see this space untouched. Please don't go inside until the police have a chance to have a look." Ally met his eyes.

"Okay." Benson frowned, then glanced at the two remaining employees. "One of you relieve Hannah and ask her to meet me in my office." He looked back at Ally as he pulled out his phone. "I will make the report right now. Okay?"

"Thank you." Ally shoved her hands into her pockets. She wondered exactly what Luke would think when he saw the empty cabinet. Could it have something to do with Mel's murder?

CHAPTER 6

As Benson ended the call to the police he nodded to Ally.

"Someone will be here soon. Come upstairs with me, I'm sure your grandmother is looking for you."

"If you don't mind, I'd like to stay. Until the police arrive." Ally straightened her shoulders. She wasn't about to let him slip into the space when she wasn't looking.

"I actually do mind." Benson looked straight back at her. "I'm sorry, but no one is allowed down here without an escort." He walked over to one of the empty cabinets and stowed the two bottles of wine, then closed it. He removed the key from the cabinet, then held it out to Ally. "I'll come back down with you when you're ready to leave."

"Don't you think someone should stay here to preserve the scene?" Ally took the key but frowned as she glanced back at the empty cabinet. "What if someone else happens to get inside?"

"The police will be here shortly, no one will have a chance to get in here before they arrive. I'll make sure of it." Benson rested his hand on her shoulder. "You can trust me."

Ally held her breath as she considered how to respond to him. She could tell him flat out that she did not trust him, or she could play along, and make it seem as if she did. But she couldn't leave the storage cabinet unprotected.

"It's right down here." Hannah's voice drifted down the stairs.

"Is that where Benson is, too?" Luke's voice preceded him as he took the final step down into the room. His eyes settled on Ally and Benson just as Benson's hand fell away from her shoulder.

"Luke." Ally met his eyes. "There's been a break-in."

"I came as soon as I heard the report." Luke held her gaze.

"So quickly." Benson narrowed his eyes. "Only a few minutes have passed."

"I was in the area." Luke cleared his throat. "Actually, I was on my way to speak to you."

"Were you?" Benson stepped away from Ally and offered his hand to Luke. "It's good to see you again, Detective."

"And you." Luke shook Benson's hand, then glanced over at Ally again. "What happened here?"

"That's what I'm trying to figure out." Benson folded his hands behind his back. "It appears there might have been a robbery. Perhaps you could help me get to the bottom of it?"

"I'd be glad to." Luke pulled out his phone. "I'll get a few techs over here to have a look. Whose wine cabinet is it?"

"It was Mel's." Ally frowned as she stepped out of the room. "Someone emptied it out."

"Interesting." Luke smiled. "You're sure none of the staff let Mel get his wine."

"I am. I am still waiting to hear from a couple of them, but they would have told me if Mel emptied it out." Benson nodded.

"Okay." Luke turned away to speak into the phone.

"I guess this tour is over." Benson met Ally's eyes. "I hope you'll let me know what you think soon."

"Excuse me?" Ally gazed back at him.

"About the wines, and the candies." Benson smiled.

"Oh yes, of course I will." Ally turned and headed back up the stairs.

Now that Luke was there to investigate the wine cabinet, she could check in with her grandmother and share with her what she had discovered. One thought stuck out in her mind as she made it to the top level of the building. If what Benson said was true, no one could go downstairs without an escort, then either someone broke in, or the thief was someone who worked for the winery.

"Ally!" Charlotte waved to her as she stepped out of the building. "I was wondering where you had disappeared to. Is everything okay?"

"Mel had a wine storage cabinet here and someone emptied it out. His wines are missing. It looks like they might have been stolen." Ally reached down and scooped Peaches into her arms. "Luke is here to investigate."

"How terrible." Mrs. Bing pressed her hand against her chest. "Who would steal from a dead man?"

As Ally and Charlotte walked back toward the car, Charlotte noticed the tension in her granddaughter's expression.

"You missed a great tour. I was pretty impressed with the guide and the vineyard is beautiful. What happened with Benson?"

"I'm not sure exactly. He was very kind to me, maybe even a little too kind." Ally shook her head as she coaxed Peaches into the back of the car. "But it seemed like after he thought about it, he didn't want to report the theft. If I hadn't been there, I don't think he would have."

"That's not too surprising." Charlotte climbed into the car. "He might not have wanted the scandal that comes along with it, since he has only quite recently started running the winery."

"But even knowing that Mel was killed last night?" Ally climbed in beside her grandmother. "Wouldn't he want to help the investigation in any way that he can?"

"He did eventually call the police, right?" Charlotte started the engine. "Maybe he would have, even if you weren't there. You can't know for sure."

"You're right, I can't." Ally looked into her grandmother's eyes.

"Wait!" A sharp smack on the hood of the car caused Charlotte to step hard on the brake.

"Benson?" Ally gazed through the windshield at him. "What are you doing?"

"Sorry, I just had to catch you." Benson stepped up to the open window with a bag in one hand. "I wanted to make sure that you had your wine."

"Oh right, I completely forgot." Ally shook her head as she glanced over at her grandmother. "My grandmother started the chocolate shop. She's probably the best one to decide which candies should go with your wines."

"Wonderful, I'm glad to be able to get some expert advice." Benson handed the bag to Ally. "Let me know what you think."

"We will." Ally flashed him a smile. "And thanks again for the wine. It's very generous of you."

"Thanks for coming by." Benson smiled at both of them, then stepped back from the car.

"Yes, you're right. Maybe a little too kind." Charlotte frowned as she drove down the road. "Two free bottles of wine?"

"I know. I'm not sure what to make of it, but I guess he deserves a little kindness. He did make an effort to try to help Mel." Ally looked at her grandmother as she turned into the driveway of the cottage.

"Did he say anything about Mel's opinion of his wine?" Charlotte stepped out of the car, with Arnold right behind her.

"Yes, only what we already know, that Mel did a glowing review of one of the wines he sent in for judging. He visited River Winery a few days ago but just because he was in the area, not to do a review." Ally carried Peaches into the cottage. "Sorry, I didn't find out more. But once we found the cabinet broken into, our conversation came to a halt. He obviously felt badly that he couldn't save Mel, though."

"Of course." Charlotte gave Arnold a light pat then turned her attention to her granddaughter. "Jeff's going to stop by, I hope you don't mind." She sat down on the couch.

"I don't mind." Ally smiled, then sat down on the couch next to her. "I wish Luke would."

"You've mentioned a few things lately that have me a little worried." Charlotte took her hand. "Are things okay with the two of you?"

"I think so. I thought so, anyway." Ally sighed. "I just worry sometimes. I thought things were pretty good during my marriage, too, and then everything changed."

"Oh Ally, I can see why you would be worried." Charlotte squeezed her hand. "But remember, Luke isn't the one who hurt you. He's a good man."

"I know he is." Ally took a deep breath, then nodded. "You're right. I have no reason to be concerned. He's just busy, and so am I, that's how our lives are right now."

A light knock on the door interrupted Charlotte before she could say another word. "I'll get it." She stood up and walked to the door. When she opened it, she discovered Luke on the other side.

"Hi Charlotte." Luke gave her a kiss on the cheek.

"Hi Luke." Charlotte smiled.

"Is Ally here?" Luke peered past her into the cottage.

"Yes, she is." Charlotte stepped aside to allow him in. "How are things?"

"Alright, I only have a few minutes, and I just wanted to speak to her." Luke headed into the living room.

Ally stood up as he walked in.

"Good to see the two of them together." Jeff

stepped up to the door just as Charlotte began to close it.

"Jeff." Charlotte smiled. "Come in."

"Maybe we should give them a few minutes?" Jeff raised an eyebrow.

"Maybe." Charlotte nodded and stepped out onto the front porch with him. "How are you?"

"Glad to see you." Jeff smiled as he looked into her eyes. "I was hoping we could sneak away for a bit. What do you think?"

"I don't know. Ally might need me for something." Charlotte glanced back toward the door.

"I knew it." Jeff crossed his arms as he studied her. "You two are trying to help find out who murdered Mel, aren't you?"

"Maybe." Charlotte met his eyes.

"What can I do to help?" Jeff shoved his hands into his pockets, then looked straight into her eyes.

"Actually, it might be a good idea to find out what we can about Mel's recent reviews and his recent travels. He was touring the area for the magazine and his book. I wonder if he might have crossed someone in the last town he was in. Maybe they followed him here to exact their revenge."

Charlotte shrugged. "We could look into his recent stops."

"That's a good idea. I'll see what I can find out from his social media postings. I'm sure there are people that like to figure out when he is in each city." Jeff pulled out his phone. "Why don't we do this over an early dinner, though?"

"I guess we could do that. Let me just let Ally know." Charlotte opened the door and poked her head inside, just in time to see Ally and Luke engaged in a passionate kiss. She closed the door quietly and winced as she looked at Jeff. "On second thought, I'll just send her a text. Let's go." She smiled as she steered him toward the car.

"See, it was a good idea to give them a few minutes." Jeff chuckled as he settled into the passenger seat of his car. "You drive, I can search."

"Yes, it was." Charlotte drove toward the diner. "Anything yet?"

"It looks like he was in a city about four hours from here for his last winery tour." Jeff shook his head as he glanced up at her. "That seems like a long way for someone to come to get revenge."

"Has his article from that last stop been published, yet?" Charlotte turned into the parking lot of the diner.

"Yes, let's see." Jeff skimmed the article, then nodded. "It looks like it was a good review. Not spectacular, but nothing that would have hurt the business. If he made an enemy there, I doubt it would have been the owner of the winery."

"It couldn't be a simple answer, could it?" Charlotte rolled her eyes as she stepped out of the car. "That doesn't rule out an enemy from the past, but it makes it far more likely that someone local committed this crime."

Jeff opened the door of the diner and gestured for Charlotte to walk in first.

"Or at least someone nearby." Jeff tipped his head toward a woman who sat alone in a booth near the back of the diner.

"His wife?" Charlotte met his eyes. "What makes you think that?"

"According to some of the comments I've read about his visits to the wineries, it looks like he and his wife didn't get along so well." Jeff pursed his lips. "She stands to inherit quite a bit now that he's gone, it certainly is motive."

"Maybe so." Charlotte sat down at a table and watched the other woman.

Jeanne pushed her food around her plate but didn't take a bite. Her shoulders hunched forward, and she kept her eyes on her food. It didn't seem to Charlotte that she was too thrilled with being a wealthy widow.

72

Ally woke up the next morning, with memories of the short time she'd spent with Luke the previous evening running through her mind. They hadn't talked about the case. They hadn't talked about much of anything in particular. They just enjoyed each other's company with the limited time they had together. After Luke had left, her grandmother had called her and told her about spotting Mel's widow at the diner.

Ally sat up in her bed and wiped at her eyes. She considered what it might be like to be in her shoes. To lose her husband, so suddenly, and in such a tragic way, she had to be devastated. She needed to help figure out what happened to Mel, if not for the safety of the town, then for his wife's peace of mind.

She prepared breakfast for Peaches and Arnold, then started some coffee for herself. She leaned back against the counter and listened to the steady drip of the coffee brewing. It soothed her racing thoughts.

One step at a time.

Who was close enough to Mel to have murdered him? According to his wife, he'd gone out to have dinner. Had he dined at the restaurant? Or had he been killed before he had the chance? She picked up her phone and dialed the number of the restaurant. Although it was too early for it to be open, a woman answered the phone.

"By The Pond. Claudia speaking."

Ally was relieved to hear Claudia's familiar voice. They had been in the same year at school and knew each other well.

"Hi Claudia, it's Ally Sweet."

"Oh Ally, I'm sorry I didn't get to speak to you the other night. I was busy with the manager and then—"

"That's okay. How are you?"

"I'm okay I guess. It's been a stressful few days," Claudia replied. "How can I help you?"

"Could I speak with Lester, please?"

"Lester?" Claudia paused. "No, he's not working today."

"Oh, okay. Maybe you could help me?"

"What do you need? We're all booked up with reservations for the next two weeks. Everyone in the area wants to try the new restaurant."

"Can you tell me if Mel Cambridge had a reservation for dinner the night before last?" Ally frowned as she wondered if she would be willing to share the information.

"No, he didn't have a reservation. At least not at first. He called and insisted that he needed one at the last minute. I couldn't fit him in, we were fully booked. But he insisted on speaking to the manager. The manager then made me fit him in. It was just for him, just one person. I had to deal with a very angry couple who had their anniversary dinner ruined, and then he didn't even show up." Claudia sighed. "I know it's wrong to speak ill of the dead, but until I found out what happened, I was pretty furious with him."

"I can understand why." Ally narrowed her eyes. "You say he didn't show up. How long after he was meant to be at the restaurant was he found?"

"Almost an hour. He'd been so insistent that he had to come in, when he didn't show up on time, I kept track of it, because I expected him to show up at any second." Claudia cleared her throat. "Of course, I had no idea what was actually happening."

"Of course not." Ally bit into her bottom lip. "Thank you for your time, Claudia. We should catch up for coffee soon."

"Yes, absolutely." Claudia's voice raised. "I've been meaning to come into the chocolate shop. Life just gets so busy."

"I know. We would love to see you." Ally ended the call, with one question hanging in her mind. If he told his wife that he was going to dinner, and made a reservation, then where was he for the hour between the time of his reservation and the time of his death? Why would he have been walking around the pond while time ticked by, instead of getting to the restaurant he'd insisted on getting into?

Ally pondered the question as she dressed for the day. By the time she took the first sip of her coffee, a theory had formed in her mind. Someone had been with Mel during that time. Maybe he wasn't just randomly murdered. Maybe he had spent close to an hour with his killer, before the act took place.

As Ally headed for the door, two sad faces fixed their pleading eyes on her.

"Oh, after our adventure yesterday you don't

want to be cooped up at home, huh?" She smiled at them, then nodded. "Alright, you can keep me company this morning." She herded them into the car, then drove to the chocolate shop.

Ally left Arnold and Peaches in the courtyard which had been set up for them with a fenced-in area and a pig pen for Arnold. She made sure they had everything they needed then went inside and started the opening routine. She turned the sign in the door to open, just as Mrs. Bing, Mrs. Cale, and Mrs. White walked up.

"Good morning, ladies." Ally smiled at them as they paraded inside and took their usual places at the front counter.

"It's a wild morning is what it is." Mrs. Cale huffed. "I couldn't even get a hot cup of coffee at the diner this morning, it was so busy. I think everyone in town was there."

"Just to gossip." Mrs. White clucked her tongue.

"About Mel?" Ally poured them each a cup of coffee.

"Yes. The whole town is talking about it." Mrs. Bing shook her head. "I'm not sure how so many people can have so many opinions about something that they know nothing about."

"I'm sure everyone is feeling a little frightened."

Mrs. Cale frowned. "I know I am. To think that someone was murdered right here in this town." She sighed.

"Murder happens everywhere." Mrs. White took a sip of her coffee.

"Don't act as if it doesn't frighten you, too." Mrs. Bing met her eyes.

"I'm not saying it doesn't, I'm just saying it's not special. These things happen." Mrs. White looked up at Ally. "I bet it happened a lot more in the city, didn't it?"

"Yes." Ally shrugged. "As far as I know." Her mind wandered briefly back to her time living away from Blue River. It felt like a different life now. But since she had returned, Blue River certainly seemed to have its share of murders.

"Oh, there is no end to their imaginations." Mrs. Cale picked up another piece of candy. "The theories are, of course the wife did it, or maybe his editor, or maybe even the owner of By The Pond! Then there are those that think he had a secret lover." She rolled her eyes. "Next they'll be listing each of us as suspects."

"Interesting." Ally narrowed her eyes, then gasped as she heard a squeal from the courtyard.

"You better check on them." Charlotte laughed as she walked through the door.

Ally pushed open the back door. Peaches was chasing Arnold around the courtyard. She heard the squeak of the gate opening. As soon as it opened slightly, Peaches ran through it and Arnold snorted in protest.

"Oh Peaches!" Ally groaned.

"Sorry." The milk deliveryman stood in the open gate. "I didn't think they would be out here."

"That's okay. My grandmother is in the shop, I better go get Peaches." Ally ran toward the gate.

Peaches didn't usually roam the neighborhood, but recently she seemed to be becoming a master escape artist.

Ally hurried through the gate and around the back of the fence in an attempt to catch her. Peaches peered at her from the end of the alley, flicked her tail, then took off at a run.

"Peaches!" Ally ran after her. She caught sight of her perched on top of a dumpster, and crept toward her. Just as she was about to wrap her arms around her, Peaches meowed, and jumped away.

"Peaches!" Ally sighed as the cat bolted out of her reach. "Get back here!"

Peaches flicked her orange tail as she slipped

through a gap in a fence that surrounded a small house.

"Unbelievable." Ally groaned. "Come on Peaches. Please!" She walked up to the fence and peeked over the top of it. She watched as the cat wound her way through a few piles of wood, then started toward the back porch. "Peaches! Don't make me come over there!" She huffed as she banged her fingertips against the fence. "Come here!"

All Ally could make out was the tip of Peaches' tail as it hovered above a few slats on the rear deck of the house.

Ally squeezed through the small opening in the fence. She shot a worried look toward the back door of the house. If the owner caught her on their property, they could have her arrested.

"Peaches!" She clucked her tongue and rubbed her fingers together in an attempt to get Peaches' attention.

The sharp sound of breaking glass startled Ally. She winced as she heard more glass break.

"Peaches, what are you doing?" Ally groaned, then climbed up onto the back porch just in time to see Peaches knock another bottle off the side of the deck. There were a few bottles to keep Peaches occupied, lined up against the edge of the deck. The door opened. "Lester?" Ally stared into his eyes as he stepped out onto the back porch. As he did, Peaches ran past Ally. She quickly managed to bend down and scoop her up into her arms.

"What are you doing here?" Lester glared at Ally as he closed the door behind him.

"I'm so sorry, my cat wandered in here." Ally held Peaches closer to her as she stroked her fur. "She can get pretty curious sometimes."

"Curious enough to break bottles?" Lester glanced off the side of the deck at the pile of glass on the ground.

"I'm sorry, I can clean it up if you have a trash bag I can use." Ally shifted Peaches to one arm.

"Don't worry about it. Everything's a mess around here anyway." Lester shrugged, then tipped his head toward the gate. "There's a gate you can use toward the front."

"Thanks." Ally took one last look at the bottles lined up on the deck. She was certain she wasn't mistaken. The labels on the front announced the name of the wine, and the name matched the wine that had been stolen from the restaurant. She was tempted to confront him about it, but she felt insecure, trapped in his backyard. No one knew where she was. She had no reason to think that he had killed Mel, but the fact that he would steal from his work let her know that he wasn't to be trusted.

"Don't judge." Lester sighed as he looked over the bottles on the porch, then crossed his arms. "Sometimes life gets hard, and a little lubrication is the only thing that gets you through it."

"I'm not judging." Ally met his eyes. "I just hope that things get easier for you."

"That's nice of you." Lester narrowed his eyes. "So, maybe you won't be so quick to make them harder on me? Anything you saw here, can just be between us?"

"Of course." Ally nodded as she took a step toward the gate. The hair on the back of her neck stood up as she walked through it, with her back to him. She wasn't sure if he'd asked for a favor, or made a threat. Either way, she didn't intend to leave it alone.

CHAPTER 8

When Ally arrived back at the chocolate shop, she let Peaches into the courtyard and closed the gate.

The cat yowled in protest.

"I know, I know." Ally sighed. "But you can't go roaming around the neighborhood."

"Where did you disappear to?" Charlotte met her at the back door.

"Sorry, Peaches took off, and I had to hunt her down." Ally glanced toward the front of the shop. "They had their fill?"

"Yes, I think so." Charlotte smiled. "Did Peaches cause any trouble?"

"It's more like she found some for me." Ally raised her eyebrows. "Lester. He's a waiter at By

The Pond. He served us. She slipped into his backyard." She filled her grandmother in on what she'd found.

"So, you think he stole the bottles of wine from the restaurant?" Charlotte tapped her fingertips against her arm. "But why would he steal from where he works? Wouldn't he risk getting caught?"

"Maybe he didn't think about it." Ally shrugged. "I doubt that he could afford to buy all of those bottles of expensive wine on a waiter's wage."

"Me too." Charlotte nodded. "So, what's next?"

"After we close up tonight, I think we should look into him a little more. He may not be our killer, but he's definitely up to something." Ally washed her hands, then began working on making a batch of candy. "Oh, by the way, those wines that Benson gave me are in the fridge. We should try some out later."

"I have an idea." Charlotte snapped her fingers. "Why don't we offer samples of the wine with the samples of our chocolates? We can let the customers do our research for us."

"Brilliant." Ally grinned. "Although we should save a bit for us, too, trust me, it is the best wine I've ever tasted. But I have a sweet tooth and I haven't tasted that much wine, I guess."

While Ally set up an area for the chocolate and wine tasting, Charlotte finished up the candies in the back. Ally had just put a few tiny glasses on the counter, when a woman stepped inside. She appeared to be in her forties, and wore a business suit.

"Good afternoon." She smiled at Ally as she walked up to the counter.

"Welcome to Charlotte's Chocolate Heaven." Ally smiled in return. "Would you like to try a few samples of our candies?"

"I would love to. I've just had a rough lunch meeting, and I saw this place, and thought, yes I need some chocolate." She laughed.

"In town for business?" Ally smiled as she directed her to the sample tray.

"Yes, my boss lives in the area and prefers to have his meetings close to home." She eyed the wine bottles and glasses. "What is this all about?"

"Oh, a local winery is interested in putting together some gift boxes that include our candies, so he offered us some free bottles of dessert wine to try out with our candies. We thought our customers might enjoy tasting them." Ally picked up one of the bottles. "Would you like a taste?"

"Sure." She grinned as she looked at the bottle.

Then her expression shifted. "Oh, from River Winery? No thanks."

"No?" Ally raised an eyebrow. "It's really good."

"I doubt it." She crossed her arms. "The last time I was here for a meeting with my boss, we took a tour of that winery. The wine tasted delicious on the tour, so I bought a few bottles to take home with me. When I opened one up, it was horrid. I thought maybe it was a fluke, so I opened the others, and they were all terrible. They tasted worse than the cheap stuff you can buy off the shelf in the discount section of a liquor store." She shook her head. "I don't trust anything that comes from that place."

"Oh, I'm sorry that you had that experience." Ally frowned. She knew better than to argue with a customer, but she doubted her story. The wine she'd tasted, had been delicious. "How about some coffee to go with the candy instead then?"

"Sure, I'll take some. Thanks."

After she'd tried her sample and finished her coffee, she purchased a few boxes of candy.

"You have a nice shop here." She met Ally's eyes. "I wouldn't get tangled up with the owner of that winery. Something isn't right over there."

"Thanks for the advice." Ally nodded, then watched her leave the shop.

The woman's words stuck in her mind as the traffic in the shop picked up. Several customers enjoyed the wine samples with the candy and raved about the taste. Ally had a few sips, just to make sure it tasted as she remembered.

"I saw that." Charlotte grinned as she stepped out of the back with a plate that had two small pieces of chocolate cake on it. "It's supposed to be for the customers, Ally."

"I know, I know." Ally laughed, then shared her experience with the customer who had come into the shop earlier. "I just wanted to make sure I wasn't missing something."

"I'll have to try some, too." Charlotte grinned and had a sip from Ally's glass. "Everyone really enjoyed the wine they tasted on the tour. I wonder if somehow she's confused about which winery she visited."

"It's possible. Maybe her tastes just changed." Ally nodded. "That cake looks amazing."

"It's my whipped chocolate ganache cake. I changed the recipe a bit. I added more buttermilk and less butter. Have a taste." Charlotte gestured to a piece and Ally picked it up.

"Yum!" Ally mumbled around the cake in her mouth as Charlotte popped a piece in her mouth.

"It is delicious. It goes well with Benson's wines as well." Charlotte took a sip then handed the glass to Ally.

"It does." Ally took a sip then glanced at the clock. "It's almost time to close up. I want to leave on time, I really want to see what I can find out about Lester."

"Okay, I'll help you close up, and then we can track him together." Charlotte grabbed the broom to sweep up.

Ally began shutting down the register.

Once the shop was locked up for the night, Ally and Charlotte walked through the courtyard. Ally hooked on Peaches and Arnold's leashes and led them to her car.

"Are you sure you want to tag along? It might be nothing."

"We know it isn't nothing." Charlotte smiled. "Somehow that young man had several bottles of wine, possibly stolen wine."

"That's true." Ally herded Peaches and Arnold into the back seat. "After I drop these two off and give them dinner, we can head out."

"Okay." Charlotte got into the passenger seat.

Ally drove back to the cottage and let the

animals inside. As she prepared their dinner, Peaches followed her every move.

"I know you're still upset with me about earlier." Ally crouched down and gave her a light pet. "You like to investigate things as much as I do, don't you?" She smiled at the cat. "But this time you have to stay home." She set her dinner down in front of her. "I need you to keep an eye on Arnold for me. Okay?" She kissed the top of the cat's head.

Peaches gave a quiet meow, then began to eat her food.

Ally watched her for a moment. Peaches had been with her for a long time, even through her divorce. Her cat was more than a pet, she was a confidante. Ally often talked with her about things happening in her life.

As Ally straightened up the kitchen her grandmother walked in from the living room. Charlotte held up her phone.

"I thought Jeff might want to tag along, but he's busy with a custom jewelry design, so it's just us."

"All set." Ally smiled as she grabbed her keys.

"I'll drive." Charlotte took the keys from Ally's hand.

"We won't be long." Ally called out to Arnold and Peaches as they headed through the door.

Once they were settled in the car, Charlotte backed out of the driveway.

Ally directed her to Lester's house.

"Good, his car is in the driveway. When I spoke with Claudia, the hostess at the restaurant this morning, she said he doesn't work today. So, we'll find out where he goes when he's not working."

"Or we'll just sit here twiddling our thumbs." Charlotte frowned as she studied the front windows of the house. "It looks pretty dark. He might be sleeping, or maybe he went out with friends."

"It's possible." Ally frowned. "But it's our only real lead at the moment."

"Lead?" Charlotte looked over at her. "You think that Lester might have had something to do with Mel's murder?"

"I'm not sure." Ally frowned.

"I don't think sitting here is going to do much of anything. Why don't we try again tomorrow?" Charlotte started to turn on the car.

"No Mee-Maw, I need to know what he's up to. If he stole all that wine from the restaurant, then he's already a criminal. Is it too much to think he might have taken it a step further and murdered Mel?"

"I'm not saying that it's not possible, Ally."

Charlotte let her hand fall away from the keys. "But I don't see a motive for him to want to kill Mel."

"I don't see a motive either." Ally sighed as she looked out through the windshield. "But I feel like there might be something there. I just want to see if he goes anywhere tonight."

"That's fine." Charlotte settled her hands in her lap. "Like you said, he very likely did steal the wine from the restaurant."

"That's it! What if Mel caught him?" Ally snapped her fingers. "The manager of the restaurant didn't discover the wine was missing until after the murder. What if Lester was stealing the wine, and Mel walked in on him? Maybe Mel threatened to tell the police, then Lester chased him out by the pond and hit him over the head with the bottle. One good push, and Mel would have ended up in the water unconscious. Then Benson happened upon him and pulled him out of the water."

"All of that makes sense as a possibility, but don't you think there would have been some kind of commotion? Something that would draw attention to what was happening?" Charlotte frowned. "I would think a chase and a murder would have created quite a commotion. Why didn't anyone see it?"

"That's a good question." Ally sighed and balled her hands into fists. "I don't know exactly. But I know I have to find out, and right now Lester is my target. So, I'm going to find out if he goes anywhere tonight. No matter how long it takes."

"I don't think we're going to have to wait much longer." Charlotte ducked down some in her seat. "I just saw the front door open."

Ally sank down as well.

"Yes, I saw him headed for his car."

Charlotte reached for the keys to turn the car on.

"Wait." Ally put her hand over hers. "Give him a few seconds to get ahead of us. We don't want him noticing that he has someone following him."

"Right, good idea." Charlotte peered through the windshield. "He's pulling out of the driveway."

Ally held her breath as the headlights swung across the car. She listened for the roar of the engine as the car headed down the street.

"Now, Mee-Maw." Ally sat up in her seat.

Charlotte started the car and followed after Lester.

He headed into Mainbry, made a few turns, then pulled into a parking lot shared between a strip of shops and the church. He parked among a few other cars.

Charlotte pulled into the opposite end of the parking lot and parked near one of the shops.

"Where is he going?" Charlotte narrowed her eyes as she watched him step out of his car and walk toward the church.

"Maybe to confess?" Ally raised an eyebrow, then stepped out of the car. "If he does, then maybe he will turn himself in and save us all the trouble."

"It's a thought." Charlotte smiled as she stepped out of the car as well. "Only one way to find out."

The pair followed him, keeping enough distance that he didn't sense their presence. All of a sudden he crossed the road and stepped into a liquor store.

Once he was inside, Charlotte crept up to the shop and tried to peek through the window. Ally stepped up beside her and peered through the window as well.

"More wine?" Ally squinted through the window as he grabbed a bottle of wine off the shelf.

"Well, it looks like he is just getting a drink." Charlotte shrugged as she watched him walk to the counter. All of a sudden he left the wine on the counter, shook his head, then started toward the door.

Ally and Charlotte were startled as he opened the door. They thought they would have more time to escape as he paid for his purchase.

Ally grabbed Charlotte's arm and pulled her down the street. She wanted to run, but she knew that would draw his attention.

Ally's heart raced as she hoped that they hadn't been spotted.

"I knew it!" A sharp voice called out from behind them.

CHAPTER 9

Charlotte grabbed Ally's hand and spun around to face Lester, as he walked toward them.

"Excuse me?"

"I thought I saw someone following me." Lester looked at Charlotte as his eyes widened. "You're Ally's grandmother." He looked past her at Ally. "Ally, who was sneaking around my house earlier today."

"I wasn't sneaking. Peaches ran into your courtyard and I was just trying to get her back." Ally stepped next to her grandmother.

"Why did you follow me?" Lester turned back to look at her. "I know you are."

"I saw those bottles on your porch." Ally straightened her shoulders. "I know you stole them."

Charlotte braced herself. Now that Ally had made the accusation, Lester only had two options. He could either deny it or admit to it. Would Lester admit to it?

"I know you did." Lester frowned and slipped his hands into his pockets. "I had hoped maybe you'd let it go and forget about it, but clearly that's not the case."

"No, it's not." Ally narrowed her eyes. "Did you steal them, Lester?"

"Do you know how much one bottle of that wine costs?" Lester grimaced. "I could never afford to buy one."

"So, what happened?" Ally asked.

"Please, if I tell you this, you can't tell anyone, please," Lester pleaded.

"We won't, unless it has something to do with the murder." Charlotte nodded.

"Okay. I used to be an alcoholic, but I've been clean for almost a year." Lester looked at his feet. "Until last week. You see they started carrying a new wine at By The Pond, Ballington's wine, and the manager wanted all of us to try it. I couldn't really turn it down without telling him why, and I didn't want him to think that I was a liability if he found out about my addiction. Plus, I figured that I had a handle on things, I'd been clean for so long." He shook his head. "It tasted better than anything I'd ever had to drink. Maybe because I hadn't had a drink in so long. So, I took more than one sip. Then I told myself, it was just wine, not hard liquor, so it was okay to take home the free bottle that my boss offered me. But that bottle wasn't enough." He looked up at Ally. "I fell off the wagon, hard. I crash landed. I'm hoping to get back on my feet and I'm going to get help, but I know I have a long road ahead of me. But I just took the first step and decided not to buy that wine."

"You stole the wine? But you work at the restaurant." Charlotte stared at him. "Didn't you think you would get caught?"

"I didn't really think about it. When you're addicted to something you do whatever you have to do to get what you think you need." Lester took a deep breath. "That night, things were more chaotic than normal. The hostess was angry because she had to fit in that wine guy, and cancel another reservation, then he was running late. Customers had been giving me a hard time all night. So, I wanted a bottle. I was just going to take one. But then it seemed so easy to take them all." Lester looked up at Ally. "Why not go all in, right? So I put them in my car until the end of my shift."

"Is that when Mel walked in and saw you stealing the wine?" Ally locked her eyes to his. "Did he try to stop you?"

"What?" Lester took a slight step back. "No!" He shook his head. "I never saw Mel that night. I stashed the wine in my car, and when I got back, everyone was going crazy. There were sirens, and Mel was getting pulled out of the water."

"Are you sure he didn't see you?" Charlotte asked. "Maybe he saw you in the parking lot? Like you said, you weren't thinking straight. You panicked. You thought he would tell on you, you would lose your job, go to jail, your entire future would be ruined."

"No, you're wrong, he never saw me." Lester glared at her. "I would never do that! Is that why you followed me here?" He took a sharp breath. "You think I murdered someone?"

"No, we just want to find out what happened. Maybe it was an accident?" Ally gazed at him. "Were you already drunk? Maybe you don't even remember what happened?"

"No, absolutely not." Lester pointed his finger at

her. "You're not going to pin this on me. I didn't do it!"

"I don't know what to think." Ally studied him. "But I do know that you did something that night that you weren't supposed to do, which tends to make me think you could be lying to me right now."

"If you want to know who killed that guy, you should look at his wife!" Lester's voice raised as he looked between the two of them. "You should have heard the way they were arguing at dinner when he reviewed the restaurant. I thought I was going to have to break them up myself."

"Mel and Jeanne were arguing?" Charlotte stepped closer to him. "What about?"

"He said something about how much better the roast was than hers. It set her off. She told him he was always criticizing and arguing with her. He tried to get her to be quiet. He threatened her, told her that if she couldn't behave, he'd have her removed from the restaurant." Lester crossed his arms. "I thought that was pretty harsh. He spoke to her like she was a child." He shook his head. "I really thought she was going to take a swing at him. She said she was going to leave, but—" He lowered his eyes. "I don't know exactly what he said to her, because he whispered it, but she sat silent in her chair after that. When I found out he was dead, she was the first person I thought of, after the way he treated her."

"Sounds like a real charmer." Charlotte frowned as she thought of how Jeanne must have felt. "You have no idea what he said to her?"

"No idea." Lester shook his head, then looked between the two of them. "Are you going to turn me in about the wine? If I lose my job, I don't know what's going to happen."

"It can stay between us." Ally searched his eyes. "At least for now. If it has no bearing on the murder I won't ever tell anyone."

"Thank you." Lester sighed with relief.

Charlotte eyed Ally for a moment, then looked back at Lester. "They'll find out soon enough, you need to be ready for that."

"I'm going to try to be." Lester nodded, then turned and walked off.

"What do you think?" Ally leaned close to her grandmother as she walked back toward the car.

"I'm not sure." Charlotte frowned.

"It looks like he fell off the wagon, and now he's trying to get back on it. I hope that leaving the wine in the store is his first step." Ally shook her head.

"The question is, is it because he did something

terrible while drunk, or because he actually wants to get clean."

"Maybe he just said that he left the wine because he wanted to get clean, but maybe he left the wine in the store because he saw us, or because he couldn't afford it?" Ally suggested. "He did steal the wine."

"He's definitely a dishonest person, there's no getting around that. But that doesn't necessarily make him a killer."

"I still think it's possible, though." Ally opened the passenger side door. "He might have been a little out of his mind when he did it. However, what he had to say about Mel and his wife makes me wonder if we are overlooking something there. He seemed so convinced that Jeanne might have had something to do with her husband's murder."

"I'm sure she claims that she didn't." Charlotte settled in the driver's seat. "But that doesn't mean anything really. It's not like she's just going to admit to it. She might have had a pretty strong motive, considering how wealthy her husband was. Maybe she'd had enough of the way he treated her." She frowned. "But I hate to judge an entire relationship over one snippet of conversation. Maybe they'd just had a bad evening, and things weren't normally like that between them."

"It's possible." Ally nodded. "I mean, Luke and I have certainly had moments that I wouldn't want anyone else to witness."

"The best way to find out more about whether Jeanne might have murdered Mel, is to talk to those that were around them the most. That can tell us if the issues between them were a common problem, or just a bad night."

"The problem is they're from out of town, so we don't have access to their friends and neighbors." Ally pulled out her phone and began to type on it. Her voice trailed off. "Well, look at this." She smiled as she held up her phone. "It turns out they have a large house and property just across state lines. From the pictures they have posted of it, they have staff working in the home. It would be a bit of a trip, but worth it I think. I'm sure if they have a live-in maid or chef, they'll have plenty of insight into their relationship."

"Good idea, but that doesn't mean that they'll talk." Charlotte glanced at the time on the clock. "We are going to arrive late, around dinner time. Do you think we should wait until tomorrow?"

"Better off going as soon as possible, I think. I think that Jeanne is still in town, so the only people at the house should be staff. They might be more talkative with Jeanne not there. Also, we have to open the shop in the morning." Ally tipped her head toward the road ahead. "If we get going now, we might be able to make it even sooner."

"Okay, let's do it." Charlotte started the car and headed off in the direction of Mel's house. "So, they were wealthy enough to have household help, but still stayed in that tiny motel in Blue River. I wonder what made them choose to do that?" She glanced over at Ally. "It seems odd right?"

"Yes, it does. Maybe he preferred to be as close as possible to where he wanted to tour." Ally skimmed through some information on her phone. "From what I can tell he doesn't drive."

"He walked to the restaurant on the night he was murdered. But the motel and restaurant are close." Charlotte turned down another street.

"According to the hostess at the restaurant it was a last-minute decision to go to dinner. So, that narrows down our possible suspects, I think." Ally looked over at Charlotte.

"Yes, it was probably someone who knew he would be walking to dinner alone."

"Which brings us back to his wife." Ally pursed her lips. "It still seems odd to me that his wife didn't go with him to dinner. Why wouldn't she join him?"

"I don't know, maybe she didn't like the food they served. He did dine with her on the night that he reviewed the restaurant, maybe she wasn't impressed. Or maybe she was too embarrassed after the scene that Mel made the first time they were there." Charlotte shrugged. "But she is the one person who knew that he would be heading for the restaurant."

"Not the only person." Ally looked at her grandmother. "The hostess, and the manager of the restaurant both knew."

"And it's possible that the couple who had their reservation canceled, knew as well. And maybe Mel told someone else." Charlotte turned down another street. "You're right, and anyone could have seen him walking on his own, too, we can't entirely rule that out. I wish I knew what he said to his wife at the restaurant to shut her down so completely."

"I'm sure it wasn't anything kind." Ally scanned the houses. "Alright, we're getting close. I don't think we'll be able to miss it, it's the biggest house on the block."

"You mean that one?" Charlotte pointed to a large house that took up one side of the road.

"How many bedrooms do you think that is?"

"Six, maybe eight?" Charlotte narrowed her

eyes. "For a couple with no children? Maybe they hosted family and visitors a lot."

"Maybe." Ally looked up at the large, well-lit house. Although the architecture was beautiful, something about it inspired a sense of loneliness within her. "Let's see what we can find out." She stepped out of the car and led the way to the front door. After a few sharp knocks, the door swung open.

A woman in a maid's uniform stared at them.

"Can I help you?"

"We're friends of the family." Ally spoke up. "We just want to offer our condolences."

"Oh?" The maid looked between the two of them. "I don't buy that for a second."

"Excuse me?" Ally frowned.

"Look, the phone has been ringing off the hook all day. Reporters have even been knocking on the door. Is that what you two are? Reporters?" The maid looked at Charlotte, then Ally.

"Actually, no." Charlotte sighed as she stepped forward. "The truth is, we're from Blue River, and we're here because we're trying to figure out what happened to Mel."

"Mee-Maw?" Ally looked over at her with wide eyes.

"So, you want to help?" The maid nodded. "That's refreshing. At least you're not after a story." She stepped aside. "You'll have to talk while I work. We have to get the house ready for the funeral services."

"I understand." Ally followed her inside, amazed that honesty had got them in the door. "We won't keep you long, we just want to know if there's anything we can do to help Jeanne. She's in Blue River, and we'd like to offer her some support. But she's hard to read."

"Oh really?" The maid laughed as she picked up a rag and walked over to the dining room table. "Jeanne is impossible to read. She knows how to wear a mask, I'm not sure she ever takes it off."

"What makes you say that?" Charlotte met her eyes.

"They weren't the picture-perfect couple they pretended to be." The maid wiped down the table, then straightened up. "Don't let the portrait fool you." She gestured to the large painting above the fireplace which featured Mel and Jeanne with their arms wrapped around each other.

"What do you mean by that?" Ally gazed up at the painting. "Was there some trouble in their marriage recently?"

"The better question would be was there ever a time when there wasn't trouble in their marriage?" The maid turned and began to wipe down the wooden trim of the couch. "When they were around, sometimes I would wear earplugs, just so I didn't have to hear how nasty they were to each other. Since they've been gone on this tour, it's been a lot easier." She sighed as she looked up at the two of them. "I know I probably sound horrible, what with Mel being killed. It's not like I wanted him dead, but I can't say that things won't be easier around here with him gone."

"Do you think that's how Jeanne feels, too?" Ally stepped closer to her. "Relieved?"

"I'm sure a part of her is. He was so hard on her. He criticized her, the same way he criticized wine. The meals she made were never good enough. The clothes she chose were never right. She tried hard, too." The maid pursed her lips. "She's no angel herself, trust me, but I've seen her sobbing her eyes out more than once. I can't help but feel bad for her when I see her like that."

"Did he ever hurt her physically?" Charlotte crossed her arms.

"No never. He would just be very critical." The maid shook her head. "I really shouldn't be discussing this, it's not my business. I'm sure if Jeanne finds out she'll want to get rid of me."

"Don't worry, it's not going to go further than us." Ally glanced at her grandmother. "We're not here to cause more trouble, we just want to know what really happened to Mel."

"You and everyone else." The maid rolled her eyes, then smoothed down her apron. "I do feel bad for the man. He thought he was invincible. His editor, Marty, warned him once that he had to dial it back on his criticisms because it made him a target. But Mel refused to back down at all. I think he took pleasure in making people cry." She winced, then glanced away.

"Did he do that to you, too?" Charlotte asked gently.

"He was critical of everyone." The maid tugged the dust cloth between her hands. "But he couldn't have thought higher of himself."

"I'm sorry you went through that." Ally crossed her arms. "It must have been difficult to work for him."

"Maybe at times, but the paycheck made it better. He kept me on because I did things the way he liked them. Now, I have to wonder if Jeanne will want to keep me or not." The maid took a breath.

"She's certainly not going to want to if I don't get some work done. You'll have to excuse me." She turned and walked into the living room.

Ally shook her head. "Poor girl. She's been put through it."

"It sounds like everyone who knew Mel was put through it." Charlotte clucked her tongue. "Can you imagine having so many people know your name and face, and none of them have a fond thing to say about you?"

"Maybe not no one. We might be able to find out more from Marty. If he was concerned for Mel's safety, that's a sign that he cared about Mel as a person. I'm sure they worked closely together for many years. It might be worth having a conversation with him." Ally glanced around the large house. "We could go digging through this place for weeks and never come across anything. We're better off talking to Marty."

"Let's make it happen." Charlotte nodded.

CHAPTER 10

As Ally watched the mansion fade away behind them, her heart fluttered with a sense of grief that surprised her. Mel certainly wasn't loved by many, but he had been an influential presence, one that no longer existed. She could feel that absence, and she guessed that the entire wine world could, too.

"If he really was so terrible, I wonder how he became so popular?" Ally looked over at her grandmother. "Why would he be such a sought after critic?"

"People definitely respected his opinion when it came to wine. He was an expert." Charlotte shrugged. "Do you think you can find the address of Marty's office?"

"Maybe." Ally looked down at her phone. "He was staying in Blue River, but I'm sure he has a fixed place of business around here somewhere. If I were him, I'd be at home base trying to do damage control." She continued to search through the information she could find about him. "Here it is! I found the address for Marty's office if you want to stop there. He might already be gone for the day, but it's worth a shot."

"Yes, it is. Just tell me where to go."

Ally relayed the directions to her grandmother. A few minutes later she sighed. "How does anyone become an expert in wine anyway? Is there a school for it?"

"There's a school for everything." Charlotte pointed to an office building ahead of them. "I think that's it. If you want to double-check."

"Yes, that's the right building, we need to look for office A25." Ally squinted at the numbers on the doors.

"Okay." Charlotte eased the car into the parking lot. "Here's the A building."

"There it is." Ally pointed to an office on the corner of the building. "It looks like there's a light on."

Charlotte parked, then stepped out of the car.

"I wonder how he's handling all of this."

"We're about to find out." Ally took a deep breath, then reached for the door handle. As she pulled it open, a burst of ice-cold air flowed out.

"He likes it cold," Charlotte murmured as she looked toward the open office door beyond an unoccupied reception desk. "Hello? Marty?"

"Yes?" A man poked his head out of the office. "Can I help you?"

"Hi, I'm Charlotte Sweet." She offered her hand.

"Okay?" Marty gave her hand a quick shake. "Do I know you?"

"I don't believe so." Charlotte settled her hands back at her sides, then met his eyes. "We are here about Mel Cambridge. We wanted to offer our condolences. We are very sorry for your loss."

"Thank you." Marty looked skeptical.

"We also wanted to ask you a few questions about Mel." Charlotte smiled.

"You and the rest of the world." Marty grimaced, then stepped out of the office. "Are you some kind of reporter?" He looked past Charlotte, at Ally, who continued to hang back.

"Not a reporter, no." Charlotte shrugged and forced a smile. "Just consider me a concerned citizen of Blue River. My granddaughter, Ally, runs a business in town, and we're all on edge about there being a murderer on the loose."

"I see." Marty flicked his gaze toward Ally again. "I'm not sure that asking me questions is going to change that."

"I've heard that Mel was likely targeted for revenge. Apparently, he had quite a few enemies. Do you think that's true?" Charlotte met his eyes.

"I don't just think it, I know it. You should have seen how thick the file of threats was that I handed over to the police. The poor guy was someone that you either loved or hated from the moment that you met him." Marty gestured for them to follow him into his office.

"How long did you two work together?" Ally stepped aside and let her grandmother enter the office first. As they settled into chairs in front of his desk, she noticed the pictures that hung on the walls. Each one depicted a cover from the Sip, Eat and Savor magazines that Mel was featured on.

"Over twenty years." Marty sat down in his chair and scooted it forward. "I was only married for five, so you could say he was my longest relationship."

"This must be devastating for you." Charlotte

frowned. "To lose someone you were so close to for so long."

"I'd like to say we were close, I really would, but the truth is, we weren't." Marty pushed aside some papers on his desk. "I tried over the years to get to know him on a personal level. I went to dinner at his house, invited him to dinner at mine, celebrated holidays with him, but whether or not he accepted my invitations, it didn't change his detached nature. I know almost the same amount about him now, that I did when I met him."

"Wow, he was very closed off, huh?" Ally shook her head. "That couldn't have been easy on his wife."

"It wasn't." Marty sighed, then folded his hands on the top of his desk. "I'll be honest with you both, I have no idea who killed Mel. But my best guess is that it wasn't a random act. Whoever did it probably has no interest in harming anyone else."

Ally noticed the tremor in his voice as he spoke. She studied his expression closely. Was that guilt that caused his brow to furrow?

"Probably." Ally nodded, then cleared her throat. "Do you know what he was doing by the pond?" She looked into his eyes. "I'm sure you had a pretty good idea of his schedule."

"His work schedule, yes. We were here to do a special tour and review of Ballington Winery. He had eaten at By The Pond before, and he'd been out to both Ballington Winery, and River Winery. He had scheduled a follow-up visit for Ballington Winery, which was pretty unusual. He usually only toured a winery once for his reviews." Marty frowned as he grabbed a small book and flipped it open to reveal a calendar. "He requested I book it right away. He didn't usually visit the same winery twice even if he was doing a special on it. I asked him about it, but he wouldn't give me an explanation, just told me to do it."

"Interesting." Ally narrowed her eyes. "Had he written his review of both wineries?"

"He'd started on his review of Ballington, but it wasn't complete. He wasn't reviewing River Winery. He just went out there to visit it. He had reviewed a wine from River Winery that had been sent in recently when he judged some wines and gave it a great review." Marty flipped the book closed. "As for Ballington, Mel often worked on his own timeline, at his own pace. I learned long ago not to pressure him, or he would become even more surly than usual."

"Had he written any recent wine reviews that

were particularly scathing?" Charlotte sat forward in her chair. "Maybe harsh enough that the owner might lose the business?"

"There are always negative reviews, but there has been nothing particularly bad in the last few months. The last two wineries he visited have been fairly positive. From what he sent me on Ballington, I assume that review would have turned out positive once completed. He wasn't the type to give five stars to anything, but he did hand out praise when it was merited." He grabbed his phone and tapped on the screen a few times before he nodded. "Yes, the information he sent me about Ballington was fairly positive. The winery is well established in the area."

"What about By The Pond?" Ally's eyes widened. "The restaurant? Did he write his review for that?"

"No, he hadn't yet." Marty narrowed his eyes. "He was going to eat there again so I presume he would have only gone again if he enjoyed his experience. But once again it was rare for Mel to visit the same place more than once, he liked to try new things."

"So, he completed his tour of Ballington Winery?" Ally tapped her fingertips on the arm of her chair.

"As far as I know he did. Like I said, he did say that he needed to go back there. I have no idea why, though." Marty rocked back in his chair. "I wish I could help you out, but he simply didn't confide much in me."

"You said he was planning on eating at By The Pond again. Would he often go to dinner without his wife?" Charlotte noticed Ally staring hard at a piece of paper on the desk.

"He didn't usually. He liked to have Jeanne on his arm whenever he was seen in public." Marty's lips tensed, then he sighed. "I guess she won't have to endure that anymore."

"Endure it?" Ally looked up from the piece of paper. "We've heard there was some trouble in their marriage. You were probably around them the most. Did you notice some strain?"

"Strain is an understatement." Marty stood up from his chair and turned to face the window. "She'd been with him for so long, and every year, things seemed to get worse."

"What do you mean by that?" Charlotte gazed at him.

"You would think, over time, a man like Mel would begin to relax. But he remained so rigid, so harsh." Marty turned and looked into Charlotte's eyes. "Sometimes I wondered how she put up with it."

"Did you ever tell her that?" Ally watched him as he sank back down in his chair.

"Of course not. It wasn't my place." Marty cleared his throat. "Look, all of these questions are pointless. Clearly, Mel upset the wrong person and they went after him for it. It's best off left to the police to figure out."

"You said he rarely went to dinner without Jeanne." Charlotte narrowed her eyes. "But that night he did, and she knew that he did. She told the police that's where he was. Any idea why she didn't go with him?"

"No, no idea." Marty stared hard at the desk in front of him.

"And where were you that night?" Ally leaned forward some.

"I was in my motel room." Marty glanced up at her.

"You're staying in the same motel as Mel and his wife?" Ally met his eyes.

"Yes, of course. This office space is only for when we are staying at home, not traveling. I found it easier to travel with Mel, that way when we needed to have a face to face meeting, I was available to him. We were putting together a book of some of the wineries he visited as well as his reviews and recommendations so there was a lot of work to do." Marty stood up from his desk and wiped his hands together.

"Are you still staying at the motel?" Ally asked.

"Yes, for a few days. Jeanne doesn't want to go home yet, she's too sad about Mel and I am staying there to offer my support." Marty walked toward the front of his desk. "Speaking of Jeanne, I should probably check with her. She's going to need to go over his financial statements with the lawyer."

"I suppose she'll stand to inherit quite a bit?" Charlotte stood up from her chair.

"I would assume so. I don't know exactly how wealthy Mel was, but he has no other heirs. They never had children." Marty picked up his phone. "Please, I have a lot of work to do. I should call Jeanne before it gets much later." He tipped his head toward the door. "You know your way out."

"We do. Thank you for your time." Charlotte stepped through the door, then waited for Ally to join her.

As Charlotte and Ally walked out to the car in silence, Ally's heart sank. Both for the fact that Jeanne had lived a life that didn't seem happy, and the fact that she was becoming a much more viable suspect. It appeared as if she had many reasons to want her husband dead, including what she presumed was a large inheritance.

The pair settled into the car. Ally stared hard out through the windshield at Marty's office. She watched his light switch off.

"We could follow him." She glanced over at her grandmother.

"I'm not sure what good that will do." Charlotte shook her head. "He's probably just going back to the motel, and I don't really want to be caught there right now. I think we need to sort through a few things. What do you think?" She looked into her granddaughter's eyes as she started the car.

"I think it's strange that he travels with them everywhere they go. With all of the technological advancements, I can't think of any reason why he would need to be by his side. Unless—" Ally pursed her lips.

"Out with it." Charlotte glanced over at her. "I know you saw something on his desk that piqued your interest."

"I'm not sure that it's so much interest, as jumping to a conclusion. I noticed a receipt on his desk for room service at the motel."

"That doesn't seem very unusual." Charlotte pulled out of the parking lot.

"It may not be, but I noticed the room number on the receipt was Jeanne and Mel's room number."

"I'm sure they shared a meal or two there, the three of them." Charlotte turned down the street toward Freely.

"I'm sure they did, too. But this receipt was for two meals and was dated the night of Mel's murder. If we are going to assume that Mel went to By The Pond to have a meal, I doubt that he would have had dinner at the motel first. Which leads me to assume that Jeanne and Marty might have shared that meal."

CHAPTER 11

Charlotte pulled up in front of Freely Lakes.

"I don't think either of us thought this would turn into such a long journey." Ally stretched her arms above her head.

"But at least we got somewhere." Charlotte smiled at her.

"Did we?" Ally opened her car door. "I feel like we only learned about how miserable of a person Mel was, and how poorly he treated his wife."

"Maybe, but that tells us more about him, doesn't it?" Charlotte got out of the car.

"It's a start." Ally walked around the car and got into the driver's seat.

"It is. Speak tomorrow." Charlotte waved.

Ally made sure her grandmother was inside the retirement community before she drove toward the cottage. She pulled into the driveway excited to see Arnold and Peaches.

Ally walked up to her front door. As she started to unlock it, another car pulled into the driveway. She smiled as she saw Luke step out of the car.

"You have a few free minutes?" Ally greeted him with a light kiss on the cheek.

"I'm not sure how much time I have, but I'm currently waiting on some information to come back." Luke followed her inside the cottage and laughed as Arnold and Peaches demanded to be greeted. "Hi, little ones." He crouched down to pet them both. "Look how happy they are to see me." He smiled as Arnold rubbed against his hand. "I didn't think I'd ever get used to that, and now I look forward to it."

"They think you're going to give them treats." Ally grinned as she set down her purse.

"That's because I am." Luke fished a few treats out of his pocket and gave them to Peaches and Arnold.

"Come into the kitchen, I'll grab you something to eat." Ally headed for the kitchen.

"No." Luke caught her hand. "No thanks, I've

had plenty to eat, I just want some time with you. Can we just sit for a little while?"

"Sure." Ally's heart melted as he pulled her down onto the couch beside him. She loved it when he just wanted to be with her. It reminded her that he didn't expect anything from her. "How are you?"

"Tired." Luke draped his arm around her. "But better now that I'm here with you."

"Me too." Ally snuggled closer to him.

"Okay, fine ask." Luke rolled his eyes and smiled.

"What?" Ally did her best to look innocent.

"I know that you want to know about Mel's murder."

"I do." Ally met his eyes. "Anything new?"

"Nothing groundbreaking, unfortunately. The only thing we found out is that Mel's wine cabinet wasn't broken into, Alicia said that Mel had come in to empty the cabinet, on the morning he was murdered. She left a note on Benson's desk because he was out but he never saw it." Luke snuggled her closer.

"Oh, so he emptied it out, at least it wasn't stolen." Ally frowned. "I wonder why?"

"Maybe he just wanted to drink the wine? Or he was planning on leaving?" Luke took her hand in his free hand. "We did find Mel's briefcase. It was found in the area near his body."

"Was there anything out of the ordinary? Anything about his reviews?"

"Just some old articles and his tablet. Nothing out of the ordinary." Luke squeezed her hand. "We've been hitting quite a few walls."

"What about Jeanne?" Ally carefully shared with him what they'd discovered, omitting the part about Lester. "So, I think there's a good chance that Jeanne could be a suspect."

"I see." Luke closed his eyes.

"How come no one heard anything when Mel was murdered?" Ally frowned. "No one reported anything to you?"

"My best guess is that the killer walked up behind Mel and hit him before he had a chance to protest." Luke shrugged. "From what we can tell, there wasn't anybody else close to the pond."

"Do you think he knew his killer?" Ally rested her head against his chest.

"I think, I don't want to talk about this anymore." Luke kissed her head. "I just want to know how you are doing."

"I'd be doing better if this murder was solved."

Ally sighed. "I feel so bad for Jeanne. Did you interview her?"

"Ally." Luke looked into her eyes.

"Luke." Ally looked back at him.

"Can't it just be us for a few minutes? No badges? No investigations? Just you and me, snuggled together on this couch, with two pairs of eyes staring at us?"

"Yes." Ally grinned as she looked down at Peaches and Arnold who continued to stare at them. She nestled closer to him. "Luke, you know how much I love you, right?" She tipped her head to the side so she could look into his stunning hazel eyes that always took her breath away.

"Yes." Luke gazed back at her. "Do you know how much I love you?"

Ally's heart skipped a beat as she searched his eyes. Was there hesitation there? Boredom?

Luke kissed her forehead, then looked into her eyes again. "Do you?"

"Yes." Ally felt warmth rush through her as she realized that she did. He didn't have to be there in the few minutes of downtime he had, but he was. The only place that he wanted to be, was there with his arms around her.

"Never forget that." Luke wrapped his arms tighter around her. "Promise?"

"I promise," Ally whispered, as she closed her eyes and listened to the sound of his heartbeat.

A few minutes later, Luke's cell phone buzzed.

"I have to go." He sighed, then kissed her gently. "I wish I could stay longer."

"Track me down when you have your next few minutes free." Ally smiled as she walked him to the door.

"You don't mind me dropping in like this?" Luke paused at the door.

"Luke, I want to see you whenever I can, for as long as I can. That's why I gave you a key." Ally stroked his cheek.

Luke smiled, then pulled her in for another quick kiss, before he took off down the driveway.

Ally closed the door, then headed straight to her bedroom with Peaches and Arnold close behind. She was tired from the wild day and wanted a chance to get some solid sleep. They all hopped up onto her bed. As soon as Ally closed her eyes, she fell asleep.

Ally woke up the next morning, feeling more confident that the case would be solved soon. She had sensed some resistance from Luke when she mentioned Jeanne as a suspect, and guessed that it was because he had some information that he didn't want to divulge. If that was the case, then she hoped that she would find out more soon.

Ally didn't want to see Lester behind bars, not until she found out more about his situation. She knew she couldn't keep it a secret for too long. If Luke found out that she'd been holding back information, he wouldn't be happy. But she wasn't ready to get Lester into trouble. Not until she found out a little more information. As she started out the door, she found her grandmother in the driveway.

"Mee-Maw, what are you doing here?" Ally frowned. "It's not even time to open the shop, yet."

"I know. But I had a thought." Charlotte stepped closer to Ally. "About something we might have overlooked."

"What is it?" Ally met her eyes.

"We looked into Jeanne and Mel." Charlotte lowered her voice. "But maybe we need to find out a little bit more about Marty. Jeanne and Mel kept a tight lid on things, but Marty might have been a bit less careful. He seemed to be quite forthcoming with information. Maybe there is something we can find out about their relationship, and the night that Mel died. Maybe we can try and speak to him in his motel room so we can get a peek inside."

"That's a good idea." Ally nodded. "We can head over to the motel before I open the shop. I have a little time."

"I thought you might agree." Charlotte smiled. "We can take Jeff's car, and I'll drop you off at the shop after."

"Perfect." Ally walked toward the car. "What do you think we might find out?"

"I'm not sure, but maybe something incriminating. The way he talked about Mel and Jeanne last night just left me feeling a little unsettled." Charlotte climbed into the driver's seat and turned on the car.

"I agree." Ally glanced out the window as Charlotte backed the car out of the driveway. She caught sight of Peaches and Arnold in the window. "I'm just not sure why."

Minutes later, Charlotte turned into the parking lot of the motel.

"I wonder if he's in there?" She turned her head toward Marty's room.

"Only one way to find out." Ally stepped out of the car. "Let's try, Mee-Maw."

"Okay, I'm trusting you." Charlotte followed behind her.

Ally walked up to Marty's motel room door and knocked. There was no answer.

"I guess he must be out."

"Looks like it." Charlotte nodded.

"Why don't we ask at the office," Ally suggested. "Let's make sure we have the right room."

Ally stepped into the office with Charlotte close behind.

A blast of cool air greeted her as she walked up to the front desk.

"Hi Ally, Charlotte." Sandy stood behind the desk. "How can I help you?"

"Hi, Sandy, we just wanted to check if Marty is still staying in room 116?" Ally took a step closer.

"He is, but he's out at the moment." Sandy gestured toward his room.

"And Jeanne?" Ally asked.

"Yes, she's still staying here for the moment. She didn't want to go home to an empty house."

"Do you know why Mel, Marty and Jeanne were staying here instead of Mainbry or Freely where the wineries are?" Ally smiled at her.

"We might have been their only option for rooms. There's a huge convention in Broughdon, and as far as I know every other place is booked up." Sandy shrugged.

"Thanks Sandy." Charlotte turned and walked out of the office with Ally close behind.

"Now, we know why they booked rooms here. I guess they had no other choice."

"Exactly, it makes a little more sense now." Ally walked back toward the walkway of the motel.

CHAPTER 12

As Charlotte and Ally headed along the front walkway of the motel, a young man in uniform stepped out of Marty's room and wheeled a cart along in front of them.

Ally walked toward him.

"Hi there, Timmy." She called out. Charlotte caught up to her and they smiled as Timmy turned around. He was a relatively new resident in Blue River and a regular at the chocolate shop.

"Hi." Timmy's brown eyes widened in recognition. "What are you two doing here?"

"We're actually trying to find out what happened to Mel, the husband of the woman staying in that room." Charlotte pointed to Jeanne's room then met Timmy's eyes as he tried to avoid her gaze.

"I see. I don't want to talk here." Timmy stepped away from the door. "Walk with me." He gestured for them to follow him.

"We're just trying to help work out what happened." Charlotte shrugged.

"I believe you." Timmy kept wheeling the cart down the walkway. "But I don't want to get into trouble. There are cameras, you know." He pointed up to a camera in the corner. "The owner installed them after the murder."

"Oops." Ally glanced over at Charlotte. "I didn't even notice them."

"Me either." Charlotte's cheeks flushed.

"What do you want to know?" Timmy wheeled the cart along.

"We're just trying to find out about the relationship between Mel and Jeanne, and Marty, his editor." Charlotte met his eyes. "Do you know anything about that?"

"I do." Timmy continued to walk. "The two of them were together. Jeanne, and Marty."

"Of course they were, they worked together closely. The three of them." Ally followed after him.

"No, that's not what I meant." Timmy stopped the cart when they reached the back of the building, then turned to face her, his brown eyes wide. "I caught them together, together. They were kissing."

"Are you saying they were having an affair?" Ally's eyes narrowed.

"Yes, I think they must have been. I walked into the room. I guess they had forgotten to lock the door." Timmy glanced down the walkway, then looked back at her. "They got such a surprise. But I got a surprise, too."

"And you're sure it was Jeanne and Marty?" Ally pulled out her phone. "This man?" She held up the phone with a picture of Marty on it.

"Oh yes, I'll never forget him. He followed me out of the room and asked me how much it would take to forget what I saw." Timmy lowered his eyes. "I promised him I wouldn't tell anyone, but that was before Mel was killed."

"Why didn't you go to the police about it?" Ally eyed him with some suspicion.

"I can't really prove anything and I've got a history." Timmy shrugged. "I don't really want the police digging into my past. I'm telling you, because I need to get it off my chest. I wasn't going to say anything about it. You know, people are going to do what they want behind closed doors. That's not really my business. But ever since I heard about the murder, I haven't been able to sleep. All I can think about is Marty killing Mel. Maybe Mel found out about their affair, or maybe Marty just wanted Jeanne all to himself. I don't know." He sighed. "Now, it's up to you, what you do with the information. But don't send the cops here looking for me, because if they ask me, I'll tell them I don't know anything about it. I don't want to get involved."

"I'll try not to bring your name into it." Ally frowned as she tucked her phone back into her pocket. Now that the relationship between Jeanne and Marty had pretty much been confirmed, she found herself even more suspicious of them. Could the two people closest to Mel really have turned against him in such a terrible way? "That was a shock." Ally settled into the passenger seat of Jeff's car.

"Not entirely." Charlotte started the car, then drove the short distance to the chocolate shop. "I suspected something was going on between the two of them ever since we spoke to him last night and you saw that receipt. Marty wouldn't have been so involved with Jeanne and Mel unless there's a good reason." She pulled into the parking lot of the chocolate shop.

"He didn't mention anything about it yesterday." Ally narrowed her eyes. "Obviously, he planned on hiding it."

"But why?" Charlotte looked over at her. "To protect their secret, or to hide his motive for killing Mel? Maybe both?"

"I'm not sure." Ally opened the car door. "I'm going to open up the shop and try to sort through this."

"I think I'll try and have another talk with Marty. Maybe he's in his office." Charlotte spoke through the open window. "Any advice?"

"You have to be careful, Mee-Maw. If he actually is having an affair with Jeanne and he suspects that you know about it, he might try to hurt you or worse to keep his secret. If Marty really did kill Mel, he might do anything to keep his secret. Mee-Maw, are you sure you don't want us to go together?" Ally looked into her grandmother's eyes.

"I can handle it, Ally, trust me." Charlotte winked at her, then backed out of the parking spot.

Ally watched Charlotte for a moment, then headed toward the shop. She smiled as a white cat with light brown patches walked over to her.

"Cinnamon." Ally crouched down to greet the

cat that rubbed his cheek against her hand. Cinnamon was a stray that had, to the surprise of the community, been taken in by Carlisle, an elderly gentleman who preferred to keep to himself. The cat had become a welcomed addition to the area. Ally gave him another pet then stood up as he pranced off.

As Ally began to open up for the day her thoughts shifted to the possibility that Marty had killed Mel. Had he been so in love with Jeanne that he wanted to protect her? Or had Mel found out and threatened to disinherit Jeanne? Marty and Mel worked closely together for years. If Marty had been walking with Mel to the restaurant, Mel wouldn't have been afraid of him. He wouldn't have expected the blow.

Ally closed her eyes and took a deep breath of the aroma of the melting chocolate. The smell had soothed her since she was a child. As her muscles relaxed, her mind still raced.

"Good morning, Ally!" Mrs. Bing called out as she walked through the front door.

"Good morning!" Ally called back, and stepped out from the kitchen to greet her, Mrs. Cale, and Mrs. White. "How are you three doing this morning?"

"We're still trying to figure things out." Mrs. Cale sighed as she sat down at the counter. "Mel's death is the talk of the town. It surprises me there hasn't been more media attention."

"Not me." Mrs. White shook her head. "Most of the comments I've seen about Mel's murder have been rather cruel. He might have been very well known in the wine community, but it seems to me that not too many people actually liked him."

"No matter what, he didn't deserve to die." Ally set three coffee mugs down in front of them. As she poured them each a cup of coffee, she took another deep breath of the chocolate aroma. "And we're going to help figure out what really happened to him."

"We have a few theories." Mrs. Bing raised her eyebrows, then took a sip of her coffee.

"Oh? What are they?" Ally smiled as she pushed the sample tray closer to them.

"I think it was the wife." Mrs. White pointed her finger at Ally. "It's always the sweet and quiet ones that do the worst things."

"I wouldn't say that." Mrs. Bing pressed her hand against her chest. "I'm sweet and quiet, and I've never killed anyone."

"You? Sweet?" Mrs. Cale grinned.

"Quiet?" Mrs. White burst out laughing.

"Well, I never!" Mrs. Bing huffed as she glared at her friends. "Please, don't hold back, tell me what you really think of me."

"I'm sorry." Mrs. White took a sip of her coffee, then smiled. "We're just teasing, Mrs. Bing."

"I should hope so." Mrs. Bing sniffed. "I think it was an owner of one of the wineries whose wine he trashed. Obviously, they would go after someone who threatened their business."

"That's an interesting theory. We did consider it." Ally narrowed her eyes. "Any winemaker in particular?"

"I'm not sure. As far as I know the only wine he recently wrote a review about from the area was River Winery, but he gave that wine a fantastic review, a nine out of ten. The only winery was Ballington. But maybe he rated a wine or toured other wineries in another area that he didn't like? And of course there's By The Pond." Mrs. Bing shrugged.

"Peter Ballington is the one who owns Ballington Winery, right?" Ally leaned against the counter.

"Yes, it's been passed down through the Ballington family for generations." Mrs. White set down her coffee mug. "I remember learning about the family in school. The winery has a stellar reputation. I'm sure that Mel enjoyed his tour there."

"We can't be sure of that." Mrs. Bing raised a finger into the air. "His article was never published. I've heard rumors that since Peter took over from his parents, things haven't been the same. Maybe he was going to write about how the winery had changed over the years. Even if it was meant to be a special article to celebrate the anniversary of the winery, Mel would always write the truth. But he hadn't published the review yet and he never revealed his opinions before the article was actually published so, Peter wouldn't have known whether the review would be good or bad."

"Let me top up everyone's coffee." Ally picked up one of the fresh pots of coffee and began to fill their mugs again. "So, Ballington claims to be an upstanding member of the community, right?" She looked at each of them as she poured the coffee.

"Yes." Mrs. Cale smiled and took a sniff of the coffee. "Oh, this hazelnut flavor is so nutty. I love it."

"I still prefer the toasted almond, but this is pretty good, too." Mrs. White took a small sip.

"Why are you asking about Ballington?" Mrs. Bing raised an eyebrow. "I know all there is to know about him."

"She thinks she knows everything about everyone." Mrs. White rolled her eyes.

"And, I'm right, aren't I?" Mrs. Bing shot a glare in her direction.

"Let's find out." Ally smiled as she added a few more candies to the sample tray. "Can you tell me a little more about him? Have there ever been any complaints about his wine?"

"Only the rumors, not about the wine, but about how he runs his company. A few years back the employees threatened to organize a protest against him because he cut their health benefits. Can you imagine? A company as wealthy as that, taking health care from its employees?" Mrs. Bing clucked her tongue. "But of course I don't know everything." She shot a glare at Mrs. White.

"That does seem cruel." Ally stepped into the back to retrieve a batch of candies for the display. When she returned, she found Mrs. Bing and Mrs. White in a heated debate.

"It's clear that the wife did it." Mrs. White shook her head. "She had motive, she could have just followed him, and ended her misery once and for all."

"Not a chance. Mel was her golden goose. There were many perks to him being alive." Mrs. Bing huffed. "Besides, they were in love."

"You two are both wrong!" Mrs. Cale laughed and stood up from her stool. "It was the editor!"

"Marty?" Ally swung her eyes in Mrs. Cale's direction. "What makes you think that?"

"He had to do all of the real work, while Mel soaked up all of the fortune and the fame. I overheard the two of them arguing at the diner the morning before Mel died. They were having quite an argument." Mrs. Cale finished the last of her coffee, then set the mug down. "Marty was yelling at the poor man. He told him that if he didn't have the Ballington article ready for him by the end of the day then Ballington might refuse to let Mel publish the special. Mel insisted that Ballington couldn't refuse, and that clearly Peter had something to hide if he tried to back out. But that Marty didn't have to worry, Peter knew that he was coming back again and he was fine with it and that Marty should just leave him alone and let him do his job or Marty might land up without a job. Marty told him that if he kept pushing, he was going to regret it."

"Wait what?" Mrs. White stared at her. "You heard all of this, and we're just hearing about it now?"

"Well, I don't like to gossip." Mrs. Cale frowned.

"Mrs. Cale?" Ally raised her eyebrows. "Are you sure about what you heard?"

"Yes, I'm sure." Mrs. Cale tugged at the strap of her purse. "I didn't want to get anyone into trouble. But Marty seemed so very angry. I think there's a good chance that he lost his temper with Mel."

"You should tell Luke about what you heard." Ally locked her eyes to Mrs. Cale's. "Will you?"

"I suppose." Mrs. Cale smiled as she looked at her friends. "Maybe I'm the one that knows everything."

CHAPTER 13

Charlotte started to drive toward Marty's office, but at the last minute she changed direction. She drove to the motel instead. Maybe he was there now. When she parked in front of it, she noticed a light on in Jeanne's room. Marty's room looked dark.

Charlotte stepped out of the car, just as the door of Jeanne's motel room swung open. Marty stepped out, straightening his tie as he did.

"Marty?" Charlotte walked up to him as the door swung shut.

"Charlotte?" Marty cleared his throat as he met her eyes.

"Isn't that Jeanne's room?" Charlotte looked toward the motel room that he had just come out of.

"Yes, I had to discuss some paperwork with her." Marty shrugged as he walked toward his car. "I've been doing my best to keep an eye on her."

"That's so kind of you." Charlotte followed after him. "After our talk yesterday, I couldn't stop thinking about how you spoke about Jeanne. I wonder if she knows how lucky she is to have your friendship?"

"I'm the lucky one." Marty pulled the car door open, then turned to look at her.

"You think very highly of Jeanne, don't you?" Charlotte looked at him. "You saw how dedicated Jeanne was to Mel, even after the way that he treated her."

"He married an amazing woman, and he never appreciated her, he neglected her. He didn't deserve her." Marty's piercing eyes were stern as they settled on hers. "Finally, she can be treated the way that she deserves to be. Mel was so ignorant. He didn't realize how lucky he was?"

"You were angry with him, weren't you." Charlotte nodded. "You hated to see him criticize Jeanne, but he did it all the time didn't he?"

"It was constant." Marty narrowed his eyes. "She couldn't breathe without him criticizing her."

"I guess that's why she ended up falling for you?" Charlotte raised her eyebrows.

"It wasn't like that." Marty crossed his arms. "Not at first anyway. We worked together so often, the three of us. At first, it started with me taking her aside and telling her not to take the things that Mel said so seriously. From there, that comfort I offered, it grew into something more. I felt such an urge to protect her. I didn't realize until it was too late that I had fallen in love with her." He closed his eyes, then shook his head. "I felt like such a fool when it dawned on me one day. Of course, then I had to face the fact that she didn't feel the same way."

"She didn't?" Charlotte frowned. "Even after how kind you were to her?"

"She was so wrapped up in Mel, that she didn't even think about what she might want, about what she might deserve." Marty leaned back against his car. "I remember the first time I told her how I felt, she was furious with me. She told me she needed a friend, not someone that would ask her to betray her husband. I apologized, but it was months before she would even speak to me again. Then, it was only a little bit at a time. It wasn't until earlier this year that she was finally willing to be alone with me again. I thought I had blown it, blown any chance at romance, blown our friendship. But one day when we were alone, she put her hand over mine. I looked into her eyes, and that was it." He looked at Charlotte. "It's so easy to judge from the outside looking in. But Jeanne wasn't looking for someone else. She was trying to be the best wife she could be. Far better than that man ever deserved. I just happened to come along and distract her. It wasn't until weeks later that we shared our first kiss."

"And how long was that before Mel was killed?" Charlotte took a step back. "How long before you two decided that he was standing in the way of your love?"

"That didn't happen!" Marty scowled. "Mel is dead because he was horrible to the wrong person! His death had nothing to do with me, or with Jeanne! I never should have told you this. I've been keeping the secret for so long now, I trust you to be discrete for Jeanne's sake."

"Marty?" Jeanne stood in the doorway of her motel room. "What's going on out here?"

"You leave Jeanne alone. Do you hear me?" Marty glared at Charlotte. "She's been through enough without dealing with some small town busybody's accusations." He looked at Jeanne. "Go back inside, Jeanne. I'll call you later." He settled into his car, then pulled out of the parking lot with a screech of the tires.

Charlotte turned toward Jeanne.

"Jeanne, are you okay?"

"Me?" Jeanne stared at her. "I'm fine. What were you two talking about?"

Charlotte studied the woman closely. She wondered if Jeanne could be capable of murdering her husband. What if Marty didn't know anything about it?

"I'm sorry about your husband." Charlotte took a step toward her. "It must be terrible to lose him."

"Thank you." Jeanne glared at Charlotte. "Mel was a wonderful man. We had a wonderful marriage."

"That's great. I'm sure you did." Charlotte smiled slightly, but her words lacked conviction.

"I can see it in your eyes, you've heard the rumors, haven't you?" Jeanne stepped back from her. "But that's all that they were, rumors, we had a wonderful marriage. There was nothing wrong in our relationship. Mel and I were going to have a second honeymoon. We would have done anything for each other." She stepped back into her motel room. "I'll thank you to stay out of my business." She closed the door.

Charlotte sighed as she walked back to her car. Jeanne could have been convincing if she didn't already know too much. Everyone knew that Mel treated her badly, and soon everyone would know that Jeanne and Marty were having an affair. It was bound to come out. Jeanne had to know that. So, why was she so adamant about denying that her marriage was in trouble? Did she just want to save face? Did she want to protect her husband's reputation?

Ally listened to Mrs. Bing, Mrs. Cale and Mrs. White squabble for a few more minutes. Her thoughts turned back to Ballington. Did he have something to hide? Why else would Mel have held his review? If Marty was screaming at him about it, and he still refused to complete the review, then there must have been something to it.

"Mrs. Bing?" Ally stepped up to the counter.

"Yes?" Mrs. Bing picked up a candy from the sample tray.

"Do you think you could arrange a meeting for me with Peter Ballington?" Ally met her eyes. "Maybe for this evening?"

"Of course I can." Mrs. Bing dug her phone out of her purse. "Of course, he'll want to see me, too."

"That's just fine." Ally nodded. "Thank you for doing it."

"No problem. I'll just tell him that you're a big fan of his wines, he loves to hear that." Mrs. Bing began to dial the number.

The front door swung open and Charlotte walked in.

"Hello ladies." She smiled at them, then gave them each a quick hug.

"Thanks so much, Petey." Mrs. Bing smiled as she ended the call. "I made us a wine tasting date for this evening."

"A what?" Ally looked at her with wide eyes. "I just wanted to speak to Ballington."

"Honey, you can't go to a winery without doing a wine tasting." Mrs. Bing looked at Mrs. Cale and Mrs. White. "Don't worry, we're all invited."

"Wonderful." Mrs. Cale clapped her hands. "I do love a wine tasting."

"What's going on now?" Charlotte stepped behind the counter and looked at Ally.

"I guess we have plans for this evening." Ally winked, then pulled her aside. "How did things go with Marty?"

"Surprisingly, he told me about the affair." Charlotte shook her head. "It was like he wanted me to know they were together. He claimed that he is in love with Jeanne." She frowned. "But Jeanne completely denied that there were any problems with her marriage. She said she was in love with her husband and was quite happy in her relationship."

"Well, we both know that can't be true." Ally waved to Mrs. Bing, Mrs. Cale, and Mrs. White as they headed out the door. "After the way he treated her, there's no way she could still be in love with him."

"I wouldn't be so quick to assume that." Charlotte gazed into space for a moment, then shook her head. "I've known women that were so in love with their husbands, they would forgive them anything. If I didn't know for a fact that Jeanne had an affair with Marty, I would almost believe her. But just because she had an affair with him, doesn't mean that she didn't still love Mel."

"The problem is, we still can't place Marty or Jeanne with Mel at the time of his death." Ally pulled on an apron and stepped into the back to prepare more chocolates.

"That's true." Charlotte followed after her. She

grabbed some gloves, then began packing some candies into boxes.

Ally glanced over at her as she added some cream to a pan on the stove to make ganache. "You remember that I mentioned that a woman was in the shop yesterday. She refused to taste Benson's wine. She said she'd been scammed by his winery before. I brushed it off as a mistake on her part, I thought that maybe her tastes just changed, but I wonder if his winery has had any other complaints?"

"It's something to look into." Charlotte closed one box and started another. "But I doubt it, Mel gave the wine he tasted a rave review and he's an expert. The wines we tasted from there tasted great."

"I wonder what was going on at Ballington Winery? Why was he going to visit there again?" Ally chopped some chocolate into a bowl. "Do you think maybe Mel was going to give Peter a bad write up?"

"Maybe, but how would he know?" Charlotte took the mocha ganache out of the fridge. "He never revealed his opinions or reviews until they were published. So, how would Peter have even found out?"

"That's a good question. It certainly would have

ruined his anniversary celebrations." Ally poured the cream into the bowl over the chopped chocolate. "Maybe Mel told Benson something about Ballington Winery when he was there."

"You never know." Charlotte rolled some of the ganache from the fridge into a ball and dipped it into melted chocolate then into crushed hazelnuts.

"Maybe I should try to find out. We're meeting with Ballington later today. But if you wouldn't mind taking over for a little while, I could run out to River Winery. I'm sure that Benson would be willing to speak to me."

"I'm sure he would be, too. But be careful, Ally, it seems like he wants a lot more than just friendship." Charlotte placed the truffle on a tray and rolled another ball of ganache.

"He may want more, but all he's getting is conversation." Ally shrugged. "Still, I'll be careful. If we can at least rule him out, then we can move forward with looking into other suspects. I think we need to find out a little more about the wife."

"You really suspect her?" Charlotte dipped the truffle.

"We know that she lied to you about her affair with Marty. So, that makes me wonder what else she's lying about. She's covering something up, whether it's just an affair, or murder as well, she's hiding something." Ally pulled off her apron and hung it up. "Are you sure you are okay with this?"

"Ally, stop worrying about me." Charlotte rolled her eyes. "It's not like I didn't run this shop single-handedly for years, young lady."

"Yes, yes I know." Ally pursed her lips.

"Oh, you can say it." Charlotte looked into her eyes. "I was younger then, right?"

"I just don't want to put too much pressure on you, Mee-Maw." Ally hugged her.

"Don't worry about me, kiddo." Charlotte squeezed her arms around her. "Besides, if I get in over my head, I can always call Jeff to help." She winked at Ally. "He's gotten a lot better at not burning the chocolate."

"That's good to know!" Ally laughed. As she headed out the door, she wondered if Benson would really be so eager to talk to her. The last time she'd seen him, he was reporting an apparent crime to Luke, who he knew was Ally's boyfriend. Either way, she would do her best to get him to talk.

While Ally drove out to River Winery, she considered whether Jeanne could be the killer. She was a petite woman, but that didn't mean she couldn't swing a bottle hard enough to harm her husband, then let the water do the rest of the job for her. The thought sent a shiver down her spine, but it also made sense. Maybe Jeanne wanted to be free to finally be with a man who truly loved her. Maybe she thought if she could just get rid of Mel, they could be together. It could have just as easily been Marty that committed the crime, or maybe they committed it together.

Ally's grip tightened on the steering wheel as she turned into the winery. Suddenly it made sense, why Mel was going to dinner on his own. Had he confronted his wife about the affair? If Timmy had caught Marty and Jeanne together, was it possible that Mel had, too? If so, he might have told her he planned to divorce her, and that might have been enough to make her snap. Her mind spun with the thought.

CHAPTER 14

As Ally stepped out of the car, she noticed a man not far from the entrance of River Winery. He appeared to be in his seventies, or even eighties. He leaned heavily on a cane as he spoke to Hannah.

"I'm sorry, but he doesn't want to see you. You should leave." Hannah frowned.

Ally walked up to them just as the man turned away. His eyes briefly met hers as he leaned on his cane and made his way back toward the parking lot.

"I'm sorry, Saul." Hannah called out to him.

Saul raised his free hand in the air but didn't turn back to look at her.

Ally paused beside Hannah and turned to watch the man walk away. She felt for him as she wondered if he could use some help getting to his car. But she resisted offering. The tension left behind indicated that it might not be the best time to do anything that might ruffle his feathers.

"Hi, Ally, right?" Hannah looked at Ally with a warm smile. "What brings you out here?"

"I was hoping to get a chance to talk to Benson. But if he's too busy I understand." Ally took a step back.

"Oh no, I'm sure he'll be happy to see you. He's been eagerly awaiting your opinions about the wines he gave you." Hannah gestured to the building. "Follow me, I'll just let him know that you're here."

Ally glanced back at Saul once more, then followed after Hannah. Clearly, Benson had time to see whoever the man was, but had refused to see him for other reasons.

Ally pushed the thought from her mind as she spotted Benson on the second floor of the building. He leaned against a metal railing as he looked down at her.

"Ally!" He greeted her with a broad smile. "Come on up, let's discuss."

"I'll be right there." Ally started up the stairs.

"Let's go into my office." Benson led her toward a glass room at the end of the second floor. It overlooked the lobby, but the angle of it provided privacy to the person inside the office. "I'm so glad you came." He gestured to the chair in front of his desk.

"I'm sorry I didn't call first." Ally settled into the chair and looked across the desk at him. "I was just so excited to talk to you about the wines."

"Excited, that sounds like a good sign." Benson grinned as he shifted in his chair. "Which one did you like best?"

"The ice wine, it goes really well with a variety of the milk chocolates, as well as my grandmother's whipped chocolate ganache cake." Ally laughed. "But both wines were very good. We heard several glowing reviews from our customers as well."

"That's just wonderful. I'll put together my order, based on your recommendations. I can't wait to get some of your products." Benson sat forward and looked into her eyes. "You're going to give me a good deal, right?"

"I'm sure that we can work something out." Ally nodded, then settled back in her chair. "But that's not the only reason I'm here. I was wondering if Mel mentioned anything about the review of Ballington Winery?"

"Why would he?" Benson narrowed his eyes.

"I'm not sure." Ally shrugged. "I was just wondering. Maybe he mentioned what he thought of the wines?"

"No, he didn't." Benson shook his head. "He never talked about his reviews until he released them."

"Okay." Ally straightened her shoulders. "I was also hoping we could talk a little bit more about Mel, and what happened to him."

"Such a terrible topic." Benson shrank back in his chair. "I'd rather talk about our future together."

"I would think you'd be concerned, and you might have remembered something from that night now that the shock is over." Ally settled her gaze on him. "Personally, I am concerned, as he was killed not far from my shop. It's hard for me to feel safe opening and closing the shop when I don't know what happened to Mel."

"I understand that." Benson frowned as he studied her. "I wouldn't want you to feel unsafe. Unfortunately, I'm not sure that there is anything I can tell you that will make you feel more secure."

"I was just wondering about that night. Why were you even out by the pond?" Ally looked into his eyes.

"I had decided to go to dinner." Benson

shrugged. "At By The Pond. I had parked nearby, and I was walking to the restaurant."

"Oh." Ally narrowed her eyes. "So, you had a reservation?"

"No, I called and they said they had plenty of openings, so I just decided to dine there." Benson frowned. "I never made it there of course."

Ally shifted in her chair.

"What about when you were walking up to the pond? Did you hear anyone else nearby? Anyone arguing?"

"Not that I noticed." Benson held out his hands. "I'm sorry, I just don't have much to offer you."

"What about the splash?" Ally locked her eyes to his. "Did you hear the splash, when he fell into the water?"

"What a morbid question." Benson curled one hand into a fist. "Ally, I'm trying to be understanding here, but I'm starting to think that your interest in Mel's death is less about solving his murder, and more about reliving a terrible tragedy."

"I'm sorry." Ally stood up from her chair. "I didn't mean to upset you. I just can't stop thinking about it. I'll go."

"What about the wine and candy pairings?"

Benson stood up from his chair. "I'd like to order some of your candies."

"I'll send over the suggestions for you. I'm sure we'll have this all settled in the next day or two." Ally turned toward the door. "Thanks for your time, Benson."

"Ally." Benson walked toward her. "I shouldn't have said what I did. It's natural to be curious."

"It's fine." Ally smiled at him. "I should get going, I have my grandmother covering the shop for me. I'll be sure to get that information to you right away."

"Thank you." Benson walked her to the door. "Ally, you know I had nothing to do with his death, right?"

"Of course." Ally stared hard into his eyes. "Why would you ask me that?"

"It's not like the police haven't questioned me about it." Benson's eyes narrowed. "I had nothing to do with it."

"Benson, I don't think you had anything to do with Mel's murder." Ally took a slight step back. "I'm sorry if I gave you that impression."

"Oh good." Benson sighed, then smiled. "Sorry, it's just with all the rumors flying around town, it's been hard not to get defensive."

"I understand." Ally stared at him a moment longer, then headed for the stairs.

As Ally walked toward her car, she noticed that Saul's car hadn't budged. She glanced around, and saw him near a small stream that ran through the property. Curious, she walked over to him.

"This is a beautiful spot." Ally smiled at him as she stepped up beside him.

"It is." Saul looked over at her. "Were you here to see Benson?"

"Yes, I was." Ally met his eyes. "Were you?"

"Yes. But he refused to see me." Saul lowered his eyes. "Life can be funny like that. One minute you matter, the next, you barely exist."

"Are you two close?" Ally continued to study him, drawn in by the sadness she saw etched across his features.

"Once." Saul sighed. "You don't need to hear my story."

"Maybe I do." Ally shifted closer to him. "I'm sorry things have soured between the two of you."

"It's worse than that." Saul ran his hand back through the thin salt and pepper hair that covered most of his head. "I betrayed him, and now he thinks he can't trust me."

"Is Benson your son?" Ally searched his features for any similarities.

"My nephew." Saul leaned forward more on his cane. "I'd like to think that I've been more like a father to him, since his father passed away when he was so young. But now, I'm not so sure." He glanced up at the building. "I'm surprised he can turn me away so easily."

"He's probably just upset." Ally shook her head. "I'm sure that once he has calmed down, the two of you can talk it out."

"Not Benson." Saul forced a smile. "He has a very particular way when it comes to relationships. Either he adores you and will do anything for you, or you cease to exist for him."

"That's rather harsh." Ally's voice softened. "If you don't mind me asking, what happened between you two?"

"I don't know exactly." Saul sighed. "I made a mistake I suppose. Benson was so excited about running this winery. The business was losing money. I warned him that businesses like this, they cost so much to keep going, and he didn't have enough funds or experience to do it. I gave him what I could to help him, but I don't have a lot of money to spare." He glanced over at the building. "Of course, he couldn't do anything halfway, so the debt just kept piling up. I tried to warn him again, not to invest so much, at least not until the business was successful and he had some experience, but he insisted that success came because of investment, and that if he wanted the business to do well, he had to put everything he could into it."

"It seems to have done pretty well." Ally frowned. "His wine is delicious."

"Yes, he has a talent." Saul gripped his cane tighter. "But he isn't doing well. Financially, he is in a very precarious situation. He decided he could fix it, by sending the wine to be critiqued by Mel. He was so excited that the review was great. He was certain that the exposure would bring him tons of cash flow and he would be able to pay off some of his debt."

"I'm sure that Mel's review helped a lot." Ally narrowed her eyes.

"It did help and his business would have continued to grow, but that was all going to change." Saul stretched his lips into a thin, tight line.

"What do you mean?" Ally met his eyes.

"I overheard a conversation. I was at the diner in Blue River, having a cup of coffee. Two men were there, arguing with each other about something. I tried to tune it out and enjoy my coffee, but they wouldn't be quiet. So, I started listening in." Saul shook his head. "I wish I would have walked out right then. If I had done that, I never would have caused this mess."

"Why didn't you?"

"Because I heard them talk about Ballington Winery which piqued my interest. I didn't hear it all because I missed the beginning of the conversation. But I heard them arguing about Mel not finishing a review. Then I heard Benson's name." Saul looked up at her. "They started talking softer, when they realized that people could hear them. But I was sitting right behind them and I started listening closely when I heard them mention Benson. I heard them arguing about him, and his winery."

"Arguing about what?" Ally's eyes widened as she realized he must be talking about the same argument that Mrs. Cale had witnessed part of. "What did he say?"

"Mel said that Benson was a fraud, and that he had to expose him. The other man insisted that he should just leave it alone, it wouldn't be good for his image. But Mel refused." Saul closed his eyes. "I knew then, that something terrible was going to happen."

"Expose what?" Ally frowned.

"I don't know. I had to talk to Benson and ask him if he knew what Mel was talking about. Benson invested all of his money into this business, and the money of several of his friends and relatives." Saul leaned on his cane as he looked out over the water. "Maybe I shouldn't have asked Benson, but I needed to know if there was any validity to the conversation I overheard and make sure that Benson prepared himself in case Mel revealed something, even if it wasn't true."

"And was there any validity to what Mel said?" Ally asked.

"I don't know, I doubt it. Benson said there wasn't. He got furious with me. He said I never believed and trusted him." Saul clenched his jaw.

"You were only trying to protect him." Ally's muscles tensed at the thought of the conversation they had.

"He didn't see it that way. He said I never believed in his business, and that I was just trying to make sure he was ruined. He threw me out of his office." Saul gripped his cane tighter. "He's never spoken to me that way before. Yes, I was furious, but it also broke my heart."

"I'm so sorry." Ally glanced back at the building and wondered if Benson might be watching them right at that second. If he knew that Mel was going to expose something about him, that gave him motive to kill Mel before he had the chance. He needed to keep him quiet. "You didn't do anything wrong, you only tried to help."

"I tell myself that." Saul looked up at the building as well. "But it doesn't feel that way. When I tried to explain, he blocked my number. He refused to see me."

"Do you think he might have had something to do with Mel's murder?" Ally tried to catch his eye.

"No never." Saul looked back at the water, and shuddered. "He could never murder anyone."

"But he must have been concerned about the conversation you overheard." Ally leaned forward.

"If he was he didn't tell me, he just dismissed it. He was so excited about the review Mel had given. He was his hero. He would never murder him no matter what was said." Saul's shoulders hunched, then straightened. "I should be going."

"Wait, Saul." Ally caught his shoulder and met his eyes. "The argument you overheard between

Mel and Marty might be important, you have to go to the police."

"And betray Benson?" Saul shook his head. "No, that's not something I can do. If only I had kept my mouth shut, he would be willing to talk to me." He walked over to his car.

Ally stared after him. She considered trying to find out more, but she had the feeling that he'd just told her everything that he knew. She believed that he'd told her, because he wanted her to tell the police, he didn't want to carry the burden of his suspicion anymore. Even if he claimed that Benson was innocent, she wasn't sure that he believed it.

Ally sighed as she pulled her phone out of her pocket. She guessed that it was way past time to give Luke an update. She settled behind the wheel and dialed his number.

"Ah, my favorite person." Luke sighed into the phone as he answered.

"You're just saying that because you know I have information for you."

"No, I'm saying that because I mean it. What kind of information do you have for me?"

Ally filled him in on Mrs. Cale's description of the argument she witnessed, Charlotte's conversation with Jeanne and Marty, as well as what she'd just learned from Saul.

"Interesting. We looked into Benson of course. But so far I haven't been able to find anything."

"I have something." Ally looked up at the building and noticed a shadow in one of the windows. "I know that he lied to me."

"About what?"

"He said that he was going to dinner at By The Pond." Ally stared up at the window.

"Yes, that's what he told us as well."

"Well, he said he called and they told him they had plenty of openings. But I know the hostess at the restaurant was furious when she had to cancel a reservation in order to fit Mel in for his meal. Which means, Benson is lying. He never tried to make a reservation at By The Pond." Ally looked away from the window and started the car.

"That's a good tip, Ally, thank you. Let me look into it. I know as always that telling you to stay out of this won't work, so please be careful."

"I will be." Ally smiled. "Love you."

"Love you, too." Luke ended the call.

CHAPTER 15

Charlotte had just finished filling up the trays to be stored for the next day, when she heard Ally enter the shop.

"Mee-Maw, I'm back." She poked her head into the kitchen. "Sorry it took me longer than I planned. I spoke to Benson, and then I met his uncle."

"Oh?" Charlotte listened as Ally shared the details of what she'd learned.

"It sounds like Saul isn't just heartbroken." Charlotte wiped her hands on a towel, then walked toward the front of the shop. "It sounds like he's also scared of Benson. Ally, I don't think you should go see him alone anymore."

"Why not?" Ally frowned. "He didn't do anything to hurt me."

"You said he seemed very angry." Charlotte shook her head. "The way his uncle spoke about him, it makes me think he can be pretty obsessive at times. I just think with his crush on you, you need to be careful."

"I wouldn't call it a crush." Ally frowned.

"I would." Charlotte looked into her eyes. "I love you, Ally, but you're clueless when it comes to just how beautiful you are. That man fixated on you the moment you showed up at the winery. If he's as vindictive as his uncle claims, then he might take your suspicion of him personally. In fact, I'd be concerned about his uncle's safety, too."

"I did tell Luke about it." Ally leaned against the counter. "He said he's going to look into it more. Hopefully, he will be able to keep Saul safe."

"I'd say there's a good chance that Benson killed Mel if there was some basis to what Saul had overheard at the diner." Charlotte narrowed her eyes. "He had a lot to lose, and he was there the night that Mel was killed."

"I agree." Ally shook her head. "But we can't overlook the affair between Jeanne and Marty. Either one of them could have committed the crime. Besides, if Benson did it, why did he pull Mel's body out of the water? What would be the point of that?

Why not just run away before anyone could see him?"

"That is a good point." Charlotte frowned as she considered it. "You're right, we need to keep the other suspects in mind. Speaking of that, we have our meeting with Ballington. We need to close up soon?"

"I know." Ally glanced at the clock on the wall. "I'd like to speak to him, and then maybe Lester again. I haven't told Luke about him stealing the wine, yet, but we can't rule him out as a suspect."

Once everything was closed up, Charlotte stepped out into the parking lot, and found Ally's car surrounded by Mrs. Bing, Mrs. White, and Mrs. Cale.

"I figured it would be easiest if we all piled in together. Right Ally?" Charlotte flashed a smile at Ally. "I'll drive."

"Well, we can all fit in my car." Ally grinned as she handed her grandmother the keys. "It sounds like a road trip to me."

"Shotgun!" Mrs. Bing shot her hand into the air.

"That's not fair!" Mrs. Cale huffed. "I didn't know we were calling seats."

"Since I am the oldest, I am the one that should get the passenger seat." Mrs. White pursed her lips.

"Sorry, you were both too slow." Mrs. Bing batted her eyes at them.

A few minutes later Ally was squished in the back seat between Mrs. White and Mrs. Cale.

Charlotte looked in the rearview mirror at them.

"Everyone buckled in back there?"

"We're good to go." Ally called out.

Charlotte started the car, then drove in the direction of Ballington Winery.

"So, I did some digging, and I did find a few complaints over the past few years, against Ballington Winery, or more particularly, against Peter Ballington. Some of the events he's hosted at the winery have turned into disasters, thanks to his poor organization. Once he even crashed a wedding, totally drunk, and hit on the bride." Mrs. Bing shook her head. "What a lush."

"That can't be true." Mrs. White peered into the front seat at her. "Are you sure that's what happened?"

"It's what I was told." Mrs. Bing shrugged. "I wasn't there myself, so I can't be absolutely sure, but many of the other complaints about him relate to him being drunk as well. I guess when he inherited the winery from his parents, many of the employees didn't have a lot of faith in his ability to run it. He's always been a bit of a partier."

"What a shame." Mrs. Cale frowned. "He had all of that handed to him, and couldn't respect it."

"Everyone has something to complain about sometimes." Ally shrugged. "It doesn't mean that Ballington did anything wrong. It could be that people have taken a single incident and blown it out of proportion."

"That's possible." Mrs. Bing winced. "But I have seen him a bit tipsy myself on a few occasions. I think the dents to his reputation might be true."

"I guess we might be about to find out." Charlotte turned down the long driveway that led to the winery. "Wow, this place is huge compared to River Winery." She peered through the windshield. "Should we have dressed up for this?"

"I think we'll be okay." Ally glanced down at her jeans, then back up at her grandmother. "I hope."

"It's alright, there's not an event this evening." Mrs. Bing shrugged, then straightened her hat. As she led the way into the opulent building, she glanced back at the others. "Our private tasting is in the garden." She greeted the woman who answered the door, then led them through the house, and out onto a well-lit patio surrounded by a lush garden.

"Ladies." Peter Ballington walked up to them with a wide smile. He wore a three-piece suit, and a slim, black hat that hugged his bald head. "I'm so glad you were able to join me this evening. I do so look forward to you all enjoying some of my wine." His eyes settled on Charlotte and Ally. "I suppose you didn't have time to change?"

"No, sorry." Charlotte smoothed down her blouse.

"That's just fine. I know how hard you must work to keep that shop going." Peter met her eyes.

"Actually, my granddaughter Ally runs the shop now." Charlotte put her hand on Ally's shoulder. "But I help out now and then."

"Oh, I see." Peter gestured to the assortment of cheese and crackers spread out on the table beside them. "Please enjoy."

"Mr. Ballington, I'm surprised I've never been out here before. Your family has owned this winery for generations?" Charlotte picked up a piece of cheese and fiddled with it between her fingers.

"Yes." Peter looked at Charlotte. "It's been well documented, and my family has done a lot to support this entire area. Were it not for the winery, the local businesses would lose a lot of traffic."

"And we are so happy to have you and your

business in the area." Mrs. Bing picked up a small tasting glass of wine and sipped it.

"It surprises me that the wine critic who was so tragically killed in Blue River, was here to visit your winery, right?" Charlotte held his gaze.

"Yes, he was. Why does that surprise you?" Peter sipped his own glass of wine.

"It just seems as if your reputation is so stellar, you wouldn't need a wine critic to boost it." Charlotte shrugged.

"He was doing a special article for the magazine and a feature in his book for the winery's two-hundred year anniversary. It doesn't hurt to hear good things. Even if I already know them to be true." Peter smiled. "Anyway, the critics come whether you want them to or not."

"Is that what you heard? That it was going to be good?" Charlotte leaned forward slightly. "Because, from what I understand he refused to publish the review of your winery until after he had visited again."

"Nonsense." Peter cleared his throat.

"Yes, I heard that, too." Ally nodded. "In fact, he wanted to come back and try your wine again, didn't he?"

"Why so many questions?" Peter stared at them both.

"We're just curious." Ally smiled a little as she stepped closer to the two of them.

"Maybe you expected him to give you a good review, simply because of your long history, and the reputation that the winery carries. Maybe, he didn't give you the kind of review you expected." Charlotte clasped her hands together. "Maybe your winery's reputation was about to be sullied and instead of a special to celebrate the anniversary it was going to be an article to signal that the winery was not as good as it once was. It's no surprise to me, since you've had some incidents lately."

"Incidents?" Peter's voice raised.

"Charlotte!" Mrs. Bing put her hand on her arm. "Maybe that's enough."

"Let him answer." Mrs. Cale looked straight at him. "Just because your family has a good reputation in this town, that doesn't mean you just get to inherit it. You haven't exactly been behaving yourself, have you, Peter?"

"I will not stand for this." Peter set down his glass of wine. "I did not invite you here to hassle me."

"Hassling, is that what you call this?" Mrs.

White settled her gaze on him. "Is that what you did to that poor bride whose wedding you ruined?"

"I did no such thing." Peter huffed, then sighed. "Alright, I may have had a little too much to drink that night. We all have our moments." He looked at Mrs. Bing. "Don't we?"

"Oh, this isn't about me, darling." Mrs. Bing busied herself with stacking cheese and crackers.

"The point is, yes, I've had my moments." Peter looked back at Charlotte and Ally. "But the good reputation of this winery stands."

"Maybe not according to Mel." Ally shrugged. "Good luck can eventually run out."

"It's not about luck." Peter glared at her. "It's about skill, and knowledge, and dedication." He gestured to the glass of wine that she hadn't touched. "Just try it, and you'll see."

"Okay, thanks." Ally forced a smile and took a sip.

"With so much pressure on you to do well, it's no surprise that you might have been quite angry when you found out the review wasn't going to be published, yet. Did you know it was going to be bad?" Charlotte looked into his eyes. "Maybe you decided to take care of the problem before the review was released."

"Nonsense!" Peter took a deep breath. He smoothed down his tie and looked at each of them in turn. "I had no reason to kill him. He didn't hold my review because he doubted my wine. He wanted to come back to the winery because he wanted to test a theory. He told me that he was on to something, but he needed my help to prove it. I agreed to help, of course, because that is the kind of man that I am." He shook his head. "Look, all of this is pointless, I didn't kill Mel. I have an alibi."

"You do?" Ally smiled.

"I do." Peter smirked. "I was hosting a dinner for the winery's anniversary. With over sixty witnesses."

"That's a pretty good alibi." Charlotte nodded.

"Yes, it is. Not that I need one, because I'm not a killer." Peter held up his hand. "I think that's the end of the tasting."

"Please, Petey." Mrs. Bing stepped toward him.

"It's time to leave, this tasting is over." Peter put down his wine glass. "I have other things to do."

As they walked back to the car, Ally heard Mrs. Bing, Mrs. White, and Mrs. Cale fussing with each other.

"We never should have come here." Mrs. Cale huffed.

"All they asked for was a meeting, not a tasting." Mrs. White scowled at Mrs. Bing.

"I don't know what you two are upset about. I had one more punch left on my wine card before I would have gotten a free glass!" Mrs. Bing stomped to the car. "I could have gotten it today."

"I'm sorry, ladies." Charlotte turned to face them. "Now, at least we know that he is not a suspect."

"But we also know that Mel was up to something." Ally frowned. "He suspected something, he wanted to test a theory."

On the drive home, Ally tuned out the bickering and tried to figure out what Mel might have been up to.

Charlotte dropped off the three ladies then headed toward Freely Lakes.

When they got there Ally and Charlotte got out of the car so that Ally could drive home.

"See you in the morning, Ally." Charlotte gave her a quick hug. "Sorry if I overstepped."

"Are you kidding, Mee-Maw?" Ally smiled at her. "You were fantastic!"

"I'm glad you think so." Charlotte smiled. "I don't think Mrs. Bing is ever going to forgive me for her not getting that free glass of wine."

"Oh, she will." Ally winked at her. "Don't worry." She got into the driver's seat and waved to her grandmother. She waited until her grandmother had opened the door to Freely Lakes before she drove toward the cottage.

When Ally pulled up to the cottage, she noticed Luke's car in the driveway.

$\mathcal{A}$lly walked up to the door to find the lights on inside. She heard soft music playing and noticed the flicker of candlelight.

"Luke?" The door was unlocked, and she pushed it open.

"Hey sweetie." He stuck his head out of the kitchen. "I hope you don't mind. I used my key."

Ally bent down to greet Peaches and Arnold. Peaches purred and Arnold nuzzled her leg.

"Of course not." Ally walked into the kitchen with the animals following her and took a deep breath. "Oh wow, it smells delicious in here."

"Don't get too excited, it's reheated take out." Luke grinned. "I was hoping to surprise you with dinner, but when you weren't here, I thought I'd set the mood a bit. I already fed Peaches and Arnold."

"Thank you so much." Ally hugged him, then leaned her head against his chest. "It's been a tiring day."

"I bet. Where were you?" Luke set a plate down on the table for her.

"I went out to Ballington Winery with Mee-Maw, Mrs. Bing, Mrs. White, and Mrs. Cale." Ally smiled as she sat down at the table.

"Oh, that must have been an adventure." Luke sat down across from her with his own plate.

"It was interesting, that's for sure. So, it turns out that Mel was on to something that he needed Peter's help with." Ally took a sip. "He wanted to check out a theory."

"Ah yes. I think I might know a little bit about that." Luke looked up at her. "There have been several complaints against River Winery regarding the authenticity of the wine that is sold there."

"What does that have to do with Ballington?" Ally shook her head.

"It appears that Benson may have been stealing wine from Ballington and passing it off as his own." Luke raised an eyebrow.

"What? Why would he do that?"

"Our working theory at the moment is that it was a classic bait and switch scam. Benson would use Ballington's wine, with his labels on it, to serve at the tastings. Then he would send bottles of his cheap, inferior wine home with his customers." Luke tipped his head to the side. "When people opened their wine at home, they were shocked by the difference in taste."

"How terrible." Ally frowned. "I guess the woman in my shop was right. But I tasted his wine, and it was delicious. He even gave me two bottles to take home to try with the chocolates."

"I guess he gave you some of the good stuff. Anyway, we're still trying to figure out if it's true. At the moment, he's looking like a prime suspect. He doesn't have an alibi for the time of the murder, and he potentially had quite a bit of motive. But just because he gave customers inferior wines that doesn't make him a murderer." Luke met her eyes. "What do you think?"

"I think you're right." Ally sighed. "But I don't really want to believe he's a murderer. He is a strange man, but I'd rather think he was a good one."

"You like to find the best in everyone." Luke

pushed his fork across his plate. "I guess that's why you've been keeping secrets from me?"

"What?" Ally looked up at him.

"About Lester?" Luke looked into her eyes.

"Oh." Ally looked back down at her food.

"Ally, why didn't you tell me the truth about him?" Luke reached across the table and took her hand.

"I would have." Ally met his eyes. "It's just, I wasn't sure exactly what happened. I wanted to find out a little bit more before I told you about it."

"And? Did you find out anything more?" Luke stroked the back of her hand with his thumb.

"Not yet. I haven't had a chance."

"So, tell me what you know." Luke leaned closer to her.

"He did steal the wine from the restaurant, but only because he went on a binge." Ally squeezed his hand. "I saw all of the empty bottles scattered around his back porch. He didn't want to tell the truth, because he knew that he would be arrested for stealing the wine, and everyone would find out that he was drinking again. He would probably lose his job."

"Don't you think he should, Ally?" Luke

squinted at her. "Don't you think he should be arrested for what he did?"

"I think he made a mistake and he's going through tough times." Ally frowned. "I guess, I'd hate to see him lose his entire future over a stupid decision."

"He broke the law." Luke sighed as he sat back in his chair.

"I know he did." Ally looked into his eyes. "But he's trying to turn his life around. Doesn't that count for anything?"

"Actually, maybe it does." Luke suddenly stood up from his chair.

"Luke? Where are you going?" Ally frowned as she stood up as well. "I'm sorry for not telling you about Lester. Please, don't be angry with me."

"Ally." Luke cupped her cheeks and looked straight into her eyes. "I'm not angry with you." He kissed her, then let his hands fall back to his sides. "I have something I need to follow up on. I'm sorry about dinner, again." He hurried out the door.

Ally sighed as she watched him go. She thought about demanding more of an explanation, but she knew there was no point. He was on a mission, and nothing she said would stop him. She touched her lips as she recalled the kiss. She could only hope that he meant what he said. If he wasn't angry with her about holding back information about Lester, then what had made him leave so quickly?

"I blew it again, Peaches." Ally gave the cat a sliver of chicken from her plate.

Arnold snorted from underneath the table.

"Oh, there you are." Ally laughed as she handed him a bit of broccoli. "I guess it's just us again."

Ally sat back in her chair and closed her eyes. As she mulled over the facts of the case, her mind began to settle. It looked as if Peter definitely hadn't killed Mel. But there were plenty of other options.

Marty stood out as a good suspect in her mind. He had witnessed Mel treating Jeanne badly for years, at least in Marty's eyes, and it seemed as if he had fallen in love with her. He wanted to protect her, and maybe he thought that killing Mel would do that. But there was also Benson, who clearly had a lot to lose if the suspicions about his wines were true and were exposed. He was also at the scene of the crime. But it still didn't make sense to her that he would pull the body out of the water and pretend to help. If he wanted Mel dead, why would he have inserted himself in his rescue as well? Maybe he got a conscience? Maybe to build his reputation within the community? It seemed awfully risky to her.

Then of course, there was Jeanne herself. Had she made herself a widow? Had she decided that she'd had enough of being in a bad marriage? Or was she terrified that he would reveal their affair to their lawyers and find a way to refuse her his fortune? She had plenty of reason to kill her husband. But no one had seen her near the scene of the crime. If she and Marty had been together at the time of Mel's death, as the receipt for room service indicated, then why hadn't either come forward to be each other's alibi? Were they too afraid of the scandal of their affair getting out? Or had they teamed up to kill Mel, and orchestrated the receipt as an alibi just in case they were caught?

Ally's eyes widened as she realized there was one way she could try to find out for sure. All she had to do was talk to Timmy at the motel. If he had brought them room service and seen them, then that might be proof that both of them were in the room at the time of the murder. They wouldn't have bothered to hide their affair from him, since they had already paid him for his silence.

"That's it!" Ally snapped her fingers. "If it was Jeanne or Marty or both, I might be able to prove it. Let's go for a walk, guys!" She looked at Arnold and Peaches, she put on their harnesses and attached their leashes. She blew out each candle that Luke had lit on her way out the door.

As Ally walked toward the motel she thought back to the night of Mel's murder. She had been so nervous to have dinner with Luke, all because he had been acting strangely.

"Wasn't that silly of me, Peaches?" Ally shook her head. "I know that Luke loves me. I shouldn't worry so much."

Peaches gave a lighthearted meow.

"I know, I know." Ally rolled her eyes. "You told me so." She laughed. She was almost to the motel, when she decided to change direction. Instead of going straight to the motel, she headed toward By The Pond. She might still have a chance to talk to Lester before Luke spoke to him and possibly arrested him. She wanted to know if he had seen Jeanne or Marty in the area as he was stealing the bottles of wine.

"I'm pretty sure it was the wife." Ally glanced down at Peaches. "What do you think? I know, it seems like she loved Mel, but what if she went so many years being put down and ignored by her husband, that she finally snapped? It just doesn't make sense to me for Marty to be the killer. Yes, if he married Jeanne, he would have inherited the fortune, too. Now that Mel was dead, Marty seemed open about his relationship with Jeanne. Would he be if he had killed him?"

"Where is he?" A man shouted from the back entrance of the restaurant. "You tell me right now where he is!"

"I'm sorry, sir, but he's not here!" Claudia stood in the doorway and glared at him. "Back off please, or I'll call the police!" She closed the door.

"Benson?" Ally stared at him as he slammed his hand against the door.

"Ally." Benson ran his hand back through his hair and looked at her. "Sorry that you had to see that."

"It's alright." Ally shrugged but held tighter to Peaches and Arnold's leashes. "Is everything okay?"

"I've just had a difficult day." Benson frowned, then crouched down to greet Peaches and Arnold. "I bet it's great having these two around. They will love you no matter what."

"It is nice." Ally smiled, then studied his expression. "Who were you looking for, Benson?"

"No one." Benson rocked back on his heels, then stood up.

"Your Uncle Saul?" Ally looked into his eyes. "I met him at your vineyard."

"I saw you." Benson crossed his arms. "You shouldn't be talking to him. He turned against me."

"Benson, I don't think he turned against you. It seems to me that he really cares about you. I don't think you should dismiss him so easily." Ally smiled. "You did such a heroic thing by trying to save Mel. I know that whatever is going on between you and your uncle can be overcome. Just try to keep your heart open."

"Yes, maybe that's what I need to do." Benson studied her with a faint smile. "You're an amazing woman, Ally."

"I wouldn't say that." Ally took a slight step back. "I'm no different than anyone else."

"But you are." Benson sighed as he gazed at her. "Quite remarkable."

"Thank you." Ally lowered her eyes. "I should be going. We were just out for a walk, I wanted to stop by and see Lester." She craned her neck toward the window of the restaurant. "I don't see him in there."

"Didn't you hear her?" Benson tipped his head toward the door. "She said he wasn't here."

"Oh." Ally stared at him as she suddenly realized that he hadn't been looking for Saul. He'd been looking for Lester. But what could he possibly want with Lester? Her mind began to churn as pieces started to fit together. "Okay then, we should really be going." She steered Peaches and Arnold away from the restaurant.

"Ally, I'll walk with you." Benson fell into step beside her. "It's not safe for you to be walking out here all alone."

"I'm not alone." Ally forced a smile. "I have my watch cat and watch pig with me."

"Cute." Benson looked into her eyes. "But they're not going to do anything to protect you from someone who wants to hurt you."

"Sure, they will." Ally pursed her lips.

"Ally, I think you and I need to be clear about something." Benson continued to walk beside her.

"What's that?" Ally glanced over at him.

"I find you absolutely irresistible." Benson tried to catch her free hand.

"Please don't." Ally pulled her hand away. "Benson, it's very kind of you to say that, but I don't feel the same way. I'm sorry. I'm in love with my boyfriend, Luke."

"The detective." Benson narrowed his eyes.

"Yes." Ally's heart began to pound faster as they neared the pond.

"What can you possibly see in him?" Benson shook his head. "He's so by the book. He doesn't get that sometimes laws and rules have to be bent in order to get what you want in life."

"Is that what you did, Benson?" Ally stared into his eyes. "Did you bend the rules? Bend the law?"

"I knew you'd figured it out." Benson sighed as he gazed back at her. "I had hoped that maybe I was wrong. But I saw it in your eyes when you looked at me. Don't be so quick to judge, Ally. I did what I had to do for my business. Not all of us are born with a silver spoon in our mouths."

"No, you're right. We're not. But that doesn't mean that we have to steal from people, hurt people. Does it? We just have to work harder for what we want." Ally took a few steps back from him and found herself caught between the edge of the pond, and his intimidating presence. Although she had begun to fit the pieces together about why he was looking for Lester, she still couldn't figure out whether he had actually killed Mel. "How could you bring Lester into your plan? He has his whole future ahead of him. Don't you worry about what will happen to him?"

"Why should I?" Benson shrugged. "He could have turned down the cash I offered him. He didn't even think about it. I told him I needed the bottles of wine from the restaurant, and he assured me that he could get them. So, what's wrong with that? We made a business deal."

"No, you paid someone to steal. You convinced him to break the law." Ally shook her head. "All you had to do was be honest. Why try to pass someone else's wine off as your own?"

"You're so sweet, aren't you?" Benson glared at her. "You're just like Ballington. You've never had to work for anything that you own. You've had everything given to you."

Ally opened her mouth to protest, but she couldn't bring herself to. The truth was, she had been handed the chocolate shop by her grandmother, as well as the cottage she had grown up in. She did work for it, but it had been easier for her than for some others who might have had to try harder to get to where she was.

"I've had a lot of support." Ally frowned. "But you had Saul. He loves you like his own son. He told me that himself."

"Like his own son. What good does that do me? How does it help me any to be the son of a man as poor as he is? He was wounded in the war, and never could keep a job after that. My father was just as bad, always throwing away what money he had. When he died, he left me with nothing. Yes, Saul did take care of me. He gave me a leaking roof over my head and stale food from the bargain bin at the grocery store." Benson rolled his eyes. "That's not exactly what I'd call a leg up."

"Maybe not, but he did at least try. He did the best he could." Ally shook her head. "Love doesn't always come with cash attached."

"I get that. But in my case, nothing came easy. So, someone like you, can never understand what I went through." Benson sighed. "I guess we wouldn't work well together after all."

"Benson, you should tell the police the truth about what happened. You have a chance to clear your name and start over." Ally searched his eyes. "I will do my best to help you."

"You would?" Benson smirked as he gazed at her. "And why would you ever do a thing like that?"

"Like you said, you never had help. I want to change that." Ally studied his expression. She noticed something sinister in it. The hair on the back of her neck stood up. Suddenly, she sensed danger.

CHAPTER 17

The sun had set. The pond was far enough from the restaurant that no one could see them. Ally hadn't told anyone where she was going. Now she was alone with a murder suspect. She'd managed to convince herself that he wasn't the killer, but as a memory surfaced in her mind, her stomach twisted with fear. Suddenly it all made sense. The reason why he pulled Mel out of the water, why it looked as if he had been trying to save him, when he was in fact the killer.

"You want to help me, Ally?" Benson placed his hand lightly on her shoulder as he looked into her eyes. "That's so kind of you. Generous, even." He tipped his head to the side as he studied her. "Are you sure you're in love with that detective? Haven't you ever considered what your life might be like if you were with someone else? With me?"

"I was with someone else." Ally shivered as his hand lingered on her shoulder. She didn't want to give him any reason to attack her, but the feeling of his touch made her want to run as fast as she could. "I was married before. I know the difference between being with the wrong person, and being with the right person."

"Oh, wasn't your ex once the right person?" Benson smiled, then winked at her. "Tricky thing, love is, isn't it?"

"It's only tricky when it's not real." Ally stared straight into his eyes. "There's only one man I want to spend the rest of my life with. But that doesn't mean that I won't do what I can to help you, Benson. You lost your father when you were young, I lost my mother when I was young. I know how it can change you. It can make you feel as if you're always going to lose everyone. It can make it hard to be close to anyone."

"Yes, it can." Benson sighed, then looked past her, at the pond. "It did for me, for a little while. Until I realized, I didn't need anyone. I didn't need to worry about losing anyone." He looked back at her. "People serve two purposes. They get me what I want, or they get in my way."

"Like your uncle?" Ally bit into her bottom lip.

"Like my uncle." Benson nodded.

Ally's heart pounded as she searched his eyes.

"Like Mel?"

"Now you're catching on." Benson grinned. "It's been a pleasure watching you put it all together. I think for a little while there, you believed me. You really wanted to help me. I can be quite a good actor, can't I?"

"Benson." Ally frowned.

"Ally, did you really think I had a crush on you?" Benson chuckled, then shook his head. "I knew who you were the moment you walked up to my winery. Girlfriend to the great detective. I figured, if I got close to you, I could keep an eye on the investigation. And you." He took a step closer to her. "You didn't turn down my attention, did you?"

"I was just trying to be nice." Ally glared at him.

"Or were you a little interested?" Benson smirked. "It doesn't matter now, does it? It's far too late for any of that. Sometimes I get so disappointed in people. Like my Uncle Saul, like Mel, like

Lester." He rolled his eyes. "They all just aren't strong enough to do what I need them to do. Mel was the worst. All he had to do was leave it alone. He had already reviewed the wine."

"But something made him suspicious?" Ally narrowed her eyes.

"It did. All of this could have been prevented. But Mel turned up at my winery out of the blue." Benson clenched his jaw. "He tasted the wrong wine. I had to find a way to cover my tracks, and quick. It wasn't easy you know. I'd been stealing wine from Ballington and rebottling it as my own. But when Mel came back after he went to visit Ballington's winery and insisted on tasting a bottle of wine off the shelf, I knew something was wrong. He asked Hannah all of these questions and I knew he was suspicious. I knew he was onto me."

"You don't have to tell me all of this." Ally stepped slightly to the side. "I should be going."

"You're not going anywhere." Benson stared hard into her eyes. "You were nosy enough to get into my business, so now you get to hear about all of it."

Ally let go of Arnold and Peaches' leashes.

"Go home!" Ally shouted at them. "Go get help!"

"Aw, isn't that sweet." Benson chuckled as he watched the animals run off. "You do realize that they are a cat and a pig, right?" He looked back at her. "They're stupid animals. They're not going to do anything to help you."

"Please, Benson. Just let me go." Ally shook her head. "This can be our secret."

"Sure." Benson rolled his eyes. "I didn't plan to kill him that day you know. It just happened. It was like this beautiful miracle, given to me. I met Lester at the back of the restaurant to get the bottles of wine he had stolen for me. That's when I saw Mel. He was walking toward the restaurant. I knew he was going back to the restaurant to taste Ballington's wine again, to help prove his theory. I knew that if he had figured out what I was up to, he was going to ruin me. He would withdraw his good review of the wine I had sent in and far worse he would expose me. I would lose everything I had worked for. I wasn't just going to lose my business. I knew I could go to jail for fraud and theft."

"So you killed him?" Ally tried to stall him.

"I had no choice." Benson gripped her shoulders tighter in his hands. "I didn't want to kill him at first. I didn't even realize that I still had a bottle of wine in my hand when I went down to see him. I was just going to talk to him to see if I could find out what he knew, what he suspected. I just wanted to reason with him. I thought if he could see things from my side, how I just needed enough income to keep the business going for a while until things picked up, he might be willing to overlook it." Benson winced.

"But he wouldn't?" Ally shook her head.

"Of course not." Benson sighed. "When I got the letter that I could send in my wine for judging by Mel Cambridge I was thrilled. Then I realized that he wasn't tasting sweet wines and my dry wines are not really up to scratch. I had to get a good review. I couldn't let this opportunity pass me by. So, I got a bottle of Ballington's wine and I rebottled it as my own. I mean Ballington's wine is delicious. It is exactly what wine critics like Mel love."

"You didn't expect him to visit the area?"

"No, when I found out that he was in the area doing a special on Ballington I doubted he would realize that the wine I had sent in as mine was actually Ballington's. But when he visited again out of the blue, Hannah told me that he refused to just be served out of the bottle of wine she opened for the other members of the tour. He insisted that a new bottle be opened so that he could have a drink from that as well, and he selected it himself. Most of the wine on the shelf was the cheap, diluted stuff I had to sell to cover the overheads. I knew if he tasted that wine, then he would begin to work out that I had been passing off Ballington's wine as my own. I knew when he purchased some of my wine that he would be able to tell the difference."

"So you had to do something?" Ally sighed.

"I did. When I found out that he had requested to take all of his wine out of the wine cabinet I thought maybe he was up to something. But I didn't realize that Alicia had already given him access to the cabinet and he had emptied it before I showed it to you. I knew that either he wanted the wine to help verify his suspicions or if he was planning on exposing me he wouldn't want to have to come back to my winery afterward, and get his wine."

"Did you know he would be at the restaurant?" Ally asked.

"No, I saw him walking to By The Pond and I tried to speak to him. I wanted to find out exactly what he suspected, what he knew. I thought maybe Saul had misunderstood the conversation he had overheard, maybe I was being paranoid. As soon as I went down there, he started asking me questions about my wines. I knew I was right, he suspected me. Then when we were by the pond he came right out and said he knew that I had sent in a bottle of Ballington's wine that I had labelled as my own to the wine judging. He knew that I was passing off Ballington's wine as mine during the tastings. I tried to show him that I was worthy of a good review." He scowled.

"He wouldn't listen?" Ally tried to keep him talking. She wanted to buy herself some time. Hopefully, someone would walk by the pond.

"No, I told him about my new sweet late harvest wine, that I'd managed to formulate into a delicious flavor. I hoped that if he had a taste of it, he would realize that I was a great winemaker and forget about everything. Then I would still have the great review and I would get the backing so I would have enough money to be able to mass produce my sweet wines. But he wouldn't listen."

"What did he say?" Ally looked into his eyes.

"He said that he would withdraw his good review and expose me as the fraud I was. He said that he would ensure that I would never have a future in the industry. I tried to reason with him, but he kept insisting that he would tell the truth and called me pathetic and a crook for labeling Ballington's wines as mine. He said he already had the articles written that would expose me. He tapped his briefcase and said that the truth was in the case and he was going to get more proof to ensure my whole scam was exposed and my reputation was ruined."

"That must have been so frustrating for you." Ally's heart raced as she stepped closer to the pond. There was no way to get around him to escape. Could she swim for it?

"I didn't mean to kill him." Benson rolled his eyes. "I only wanted him to listen. I thought if I hit him with the bottle he would just keep quiet, just for a second. But I guess I hit him much harder than I intended. He fell back into the water and started sinking. I pulled him out as fast as I could, but it was too late. He had swallowed too much water."

"Did you?" Ally locked her eyes to his. "Did you really try to help him? Or did you just look through all of his pockets for the key to his briefcase? You thought if you could get the key, you could get any documentation he made about your scam. You made it look like you were helping him, but really you were searching him. Weren't you?"

"Yes, I needed that paperwork." Benson scowled.

"Why didn't you just steal the whole briefcase?" Ally asked.

"Hannah told me that when he was at the wine tasting at my vineyard, he misplaced the briefcase. He had a tablet inside, and he managed to use his locating device on his phone and tablet to find the briefcase. Apparently, he often misplaced it. So, I knew if I stole it they would be able to find it and it would lead straight to me as the one that took it."

"Did you manage to get the papers out of the briefcase?" Ally tried to steady her breathing.

"Yes, he dropped the briefcase when I hit him. I threw it into some brush. I managed to find it, open it and get out the papers before the police located it."

Benson took a step back and covered his face with his hands.

"This isn't me!" He shrieked as he dug his fingers into his hair. "This isn't me! I'm not a killer!"

Ally saw her chance as he kept his hands pressed against his face. She knew that if she tried to run in either direction he would easily tackle her into the water. Her only option was to do something that would take him by surprise and give her at least a few seconds of a head start.

Ally took a deep breath, then turned and jumped

into the water. The cold shocked her more than the splash. She hadn't expected it to be quite so freezing. It took her breath away. She surfaced quickly and drew down another breath as her heart raced. As she swam through the murky liquid, she tried not to think about what might be swimming beside her. Snakes? Leeches? The pond wasn't meant for swimming in. Water splashed behind her, droplets struck her head as she came up for air again. Behind her, she saw Benson, thrashing toward her.

"No, no!" Ally's muscles ached as she swam faster.

Ally knew that she had to swim faster than him, or he would pull her down under the water. Already she regretted her decision to jump into the pond. She knew that she hadn't told anyone where she was. No one would even know that she was missing. She had to swim as fast as she could, otherwise, she might never be found. The thought of her grandmother and Luke going through that kind of pain made her weak with fear. She squeezed her eyes shut and dove back under the water. She had to swim harder, faster. The pond wasn't that big. All she had to do was make it to the other side before he could reach her. But the cold temperature sank into her skin, and her muscles. It sapped her energy faster than she could imagine possible. She knew how to swim, but in her panic, she felt as if she couldn't remember how to keep herself afloat. She broke through the surface for another breath of air. As she looked back over her shoulder, she expected to see Benson right behind her.

Instead she saw nothing but calm water. Her eyes widened as she hoped that maybe he had given up on trying to catch her. She allowed herself to take an extra breath. Suddenly she felt arms around her legs, tugging down.

"No!" Ally tried to scream, but the water filled her mouth before she could get the sound out. She jerked and kicked her legs as hard as she could. When she felt him let go, she swam forward. She ignored the pain in her arms and legs, she ignored the ache in her lungs as they became desperate for air. She kept swimming until she started to feel the water get a little more shallow. Only then did she allow herself to surface. She looked back over her shoulder just in time to see Benson disappear through the trees near the pond. He'd given up. He'd run off. She felt a rush of relief. But when she picked her arm up to swim, it sank back down into the water. He'd run off because he thought he'd finished the job. She'd stayed under the water so long, that he thought she wasn't coming back up. She'd stayed under too long. Her body couldn't recover from the cold and the exhaustion.

Ally's head began to slip under the water. She'd exhausted herself so much from swimming away from Benson, that she didn't have much strength left to get to the edge of the pond. As she took in a deep breath, she sank down lower in the water. She focused on the shore, which wasn't very far, and tried to coax her muscles into moving. However, the panic she had experienced as she fought with Benson left her feeling very weak.

"Help!" Ally held one hand up out of the water as she felt herself sink again. She closed her eyes as the murky water covered her face. Oddly, despite the cold temperature of the water, she began to feel warm.

A sharp bump against her stomach made her stir enough to push her head up above the water again. She felt the bump against her stomach again. She pulled herself farther up out of the water and took a breath of fresh air. Just then a small head poked up out of the water. Arnold looked up at her with wide eyes and snorted.

"Arnold?" Ally stared at him, still too exhausted to swim.

Arnold snorted again and nudged her arm.

Ally closed her eyes as fatigue threatened to take over her again. Pain rippled through her body. She managed to stretch out on her back, and felt Arnold nudge his head against her arm again. As she floated in the cold water she wondered if she would make it to the shore. It wasn't far, and she wanted to swim, but her body simply wouldn't cooperate. It was hard to think straight. She gazed at the stars that spread out across the sky above her. Maybe it was okay to just rest for a little while. Maybe she would regain some strength if she could just close her eyes for a few minutes. She continued to feel Arnold's nudging. Soon she felt mud and sludge against her arms. She became aware that she wasn't floating anymore. Arnold had managed to guide her toward the edge of the pond. She could feel his snout poking at her cheeks and hands. But she couldn't open her eyes. Cold sludge still clung to her as she remained half in and half out of the water, right at the edge of the pond.

"Ally!" She heard her name called out. It sounded strange, as if it was very far away, or muffled by something thick and woolly. "Ally!" She heard it again, and this time she knew the voice who shouted it. Her chest ached as she wished she could answer him. If she could just call out to him, he would find her. But she couldn't get her mouth to move. She couldn't get her eyes to open. Benson was right to run off. He had already finished the job. It was too late for her.

CHAPTER 18

Someone pulled Ally out of the water. She felt the mud drag along her skin. She heard Arnold's snort.

"Ally, wake up!" Luke's voice, right beside her.

Ally felt hands on her shoulders. She felt him shaking her.

"Ally, wake up! Please wake up!"

She tried to force her eyes open, but she felt too tired to do anything.

A sharp sting landed across her cheek. She sucked in a breath and opened her eyes.

"Did you slap me?" Ally mumbled as she stared up at Luke.

"I'm so sorry, I had to." Tears filled his eyes as

he propped her up against his chest. "We need to get you warm."

Ally felt him wrap his jacket around her shoulders, and something else drape over her legs. When she opened her eyes again, she saw that he'd taken off his shirt to cover her.

"Luke, you'll be cold." Ally leaned her head against his chest.

"The ambulance is almost here." Luke held her close. "Are you okay? Are you hurt?"

"I'm okay." Ally shook her head. "I just got so tired and cold." She began to feel stronger as she warmed up from his body heat and the jacket and shirt draped over her. "Benson!" She looked up at Luke. "You have to catch him! He ran off into the woods!"

"Don't worry." Luke held her close. "We already have him in custody. I heard the call over the radio on my way here."

"How did you know?" Ally stared into his eyes.

"I brought Lester in for questioning, and he told me everything, about how Benson was using the bottles of wine he stole to pass off as his own. He said that he stole the bottles of wine for Benson but landed up drinking some of them. He didn't fall off the wagon because he tasted the wine, he fell off because he knew that Benson had killed Mel. Lester saw Benson had a bottle of the wine in his hand when he went down to the pond. He knew that he was wearing gloves because he had helped Lester steal the wine. He had let him into the back of the restaurant. When Lester found out how Mel had died, he knew Benson must have killed him. Once Lester told me that, I knew I had to find Benson. We got a call from By The Pond, saying that Benson had been there causing a commotion and they wanted a restraining order. So, I came down here to see if he was here. That's when I saw you, and Arnold." He took a sharp breath as he looked down at the pig. "I think he saved you."

"I know he did." Ally ran her hand along Arnold's back. "I don't know how he managed it, but he saved me."

"Shh, you should rest." Luke caressed her cheek with his palm.

"I'm okay now." Ally sat up some. "I feel stronger. I just got winded in the water. I'll be okay." She looked into his eyes. "Just stay with me, okay? I know you should go and talk to Benson, I know that you have paperwork to file, but please just stay with me. Just for a bit at least." She wrapped her arms around him.

"I'm not going anywhere, Ally." Luke kissed the top of her head. Then he shivered.

"I knew you'd get cold." Ally frowned. "Take your jacket back, I'll be fine."

"I'm not cold, Ally. That's not it." Luke frowned. "I know this might not be the right time. It never feels like the right time. But Ally, I can't wait any longer." Luke pulled her close to him and brushed her damp hair away from her cheeks. "I'm so sorry that all of this happened. I'm sorry I wasn't here to protect you."

"Luke, you came right when I needed you." Ally looked into his eyes. "What are you waiting for?"

"I had so many ideas. I couldn't pick just one. And then, I finally did." Luke shook his head. "But I blew it. I've been trying to come up with something new, something even better. But I can't spend another minute without doing this." He took her hand and shifted his body until he had one knee on the ground, and one bent.

"Luke, it's okay. Whatever it is." Ally smiled at him as she studied him. "I love you, you know. I know you love me, too. Whatever it is, we can figure it out."

"Ally." Luke stared into her eyes. "Every moment we've spent together has been amazing.

From the first moment I met you, I knew. I felt a spark between us. I didn't understand it at first, but I knew it was different from anything I had ever felt before."

"Luke?" Ally took a sharp breath as he tightened his grasp on her hand.

"Ally, I want to spend the rest of my life with you. I know, we have to shuffle our schedules sometimes to get the time we need together, but we always make it work. I know, we don't always agree on things, but that only makes me love you more. Ally, will you marry me?" Luke slipped a box from his pocket and held it out to her.

Ally felt faint as she stared at the box. She thought back to the beautiful sundress she'd worn to dinner. As she recalled him falling on one knee, she realized he hadn't tripped at all. He had intended to propose. Now, here she was, dripping pond scum, with a good amount of mud on areas of her body that she'd never had mud on before. Still, he looked at her as if she was the most beautiful woman he'd ever seen.

"Oh Ally!" Charlotte gasped from a few feet away, then covered her mouth. Mrs. Bing, Mrs. Cale and Mrs. White stood next to her. Peaches wound her way around Charlotte's legs and purred.

Ally realized she must have gone to find her grandmother, to try to get help for her.

"Ally?" Luke shivered again. He looked into her eyes. "It's okay if you aren't ready. You can tell me no if that's what you want. I never should have asked you now, you need an ambulance not an engagement ring, what was I thinking?" He winced as he shook his head.

"Luke!" Ally laughed as she grabbed his cheeks and pulled him in for a passionate kiss. Once she broke free of it, she looked into his eyes. "Yes, Luke, I will marry you. I would marry you even if we were in the middle of the desert. I would marry you even if we were stranded on an island. All you had to do was ask!"

"Really?" Luke's hands trembled as he opened the ring box.

Ally smiled at the sight of the ring.

"Luke, I always imagined this moment. Not a perfect moment, not the right moment, just the moment when you would ask. There is no question in my mind that you are the person I want to spend the rest of my life with. Whether we are married or not I want to spend my life with you. I love you."

As she kissed him again, a snout pressed up against her elbow. A set of paws kneaded at her knee. She heard her grandmother digging in her purse for a tissue. Mrs. Bing, Mrs. Cale and Mrs. White clapped happily. No, it wasn't perfect, but she had never felt more loved, and that made it the best moment of her life.

The End

WHIPPED CHOCOLATE GANACHE CAKE RECIPE

Ingredients:

Cake

2 sticks (1 cup) butter

2 1/4 cups all-purpose flour

2/3 cup unsweetened cocoa powder

1 teaspoon baking soda

1 3/4 cups superfine sugar

4 eggs

1 teaspoon vanilla extract

1 cup milk

Whipped Chocolate Ganache

14 ounces semi-sweet chocolate

2 cups heavy cream

Preparation:

Preheat the oven to 350 degrees Fahrenheit.

Butter and line the base of 2 x 9-inch round cake pans.

Melt the butter and leave aside to cool.

Sift the flour, cocoa powder and baking soda into a mixing bowl. Mix together.

Add the superfine sugar. Mix together.

Mix in the melted butter, scraping down the sides.

Lightly beat the eggs in a bowl. Gradually add the eggs to the mixture, mixing until well-combined.

Mix in the vanilla extract.

Gradually mix in the milk, frequently scraping down the sides of the bowl.

Divide the mixture between the prepared cake pans.

Bake in the pre-heated oven for 20-25 minutes, until a skewer inserted into the middle comes out clean.

Leave the cakes to cool in the cake pans for about 10 minutes and then remove from the pans and cool on a wire rack. Once cooled remove parchment paper from the base of the cakes.

To make the whipped ganache, break up the chocolate into pieces and place in a heatproof bowl. Heat up the cream until it just starts to bubble around the edges. Do not let it come to the boil. Pour over the chocolate and leave aside for about 10 minutes. Then stir until the cream and the chocolate are well-combined. Place in the refrigerator and stir about every 10 minutes. When the ganache is cool to the touch remove from the refrigerator and whisk until the mixture becomes light and fluffy. Be careful not to overwhip.

Top one of the cakes with the whipped ganache and place the other on top. Spread the whipped ganache over the tops and sides of the cake.

Place the cake in the refrigerator for the ganache to set.

Remove from the refrigerator and leave at room temperature for about 20 minutes before eating.

Enjoy!!

Christmas Cookies and Criminals

DUNE HOUSE COZY MYSTERIES

Seaside Secrets

Boats and Bad Guys

Treasured History

Hidden Hideaways

Dodgy Dealings

Suspects and Surprises

Ruffled Feathers

A Fishy Discovery

Danger in the Depths

Celebrities and Chaos

Pups, Pilots and Peril

Tides, Trails and Trouble

Racing and Robberies

Athletes and Alibis

Manuscripts and Deadly Motives

Pelicans, Pier and Poison

Sand, Sea and a Skeleton

Pianos and Prison

WAGGING TAIL COZY MYSTERIES

Murder at Pawprint Creek (prequel)

Murder at Pooch Park

Murder at the Pet Boutique

A Merry Murder at St. Bernard Cabins

Murder at the Dog Training Academy

Murder at Corgi Country Club

A Merry Murder on Ruff Road

Murder at Poodle Place

Murder at Hound Hill

Murder at Rover Meadows

SAGE GARDENS COZY MYSTERIES

Sage Gardens Cozy Mystery Series Box Set Volume 1 (Books 1 - 4)

Birthdays Can Be Deadly

Money Can Be Deadly

Trust Can Be Deadly

Ties Can Be Deadly

Rocks Can Be Deadly

Jewelry Can Be Deadly

Numbers Can Be Deadly

Memories Can Be Deadly

Paintings Can Be Deadly

Snow Can Be Deadly

Tea Can Be Deadly

Greed Can Be Deadly

Clutter Can Be Deadly

NUTS ABOUT NUTS COZY MYSTERIES

A Tough Case to Crack

A Seed of Doubt

Roasted Peanuts and Peril

Chestnuts, Camping and Culprits

DONUT TRUCK COZY MYSTERIES

Deadly Deals and Donuts

Fatal Festive Donuts

Bunny Donuts and a Body

Strawberry Donuts and Scandal

Frosted Donuts and Fatal Falls

BEKKI THE BEAUTICIAN COZY MYSTERIES

Hairspray and Homicide

A Dyed Blonde and a Dead Body

Mascara and Murder

Pageant and Poison

Conditioner and a Corpse

Mistletoe, Makeup and Murder

Hairpin, Hair Dryer and Homicide

Blush, a Bride and a Body

Shampoo and a Stiff

Cosmetics, a Cruise and a Killer

Lipstick, a Long Iron and Lifeless

Camping, Concealer and Criminals

Treated and Dyed

A Wrinkle-Free Murder

A MACARON PATISSERIE COZY MYSTERY SERIES

Sifting for Suspects

Recipes and Revenge

Mansions, Macarons and Murder

HEAVENLY HIGHLAND INN COZY MYSTERIES

Murdering the Roses

Dead in the Daisies

Killing the Carnations

Drowning the Daffodils

Suffocating the Sunflowers

Books, Bullets and Blooms

A Deadly Serious Gardening Contest

A Bridal Bouquet and a Body

Digging for Dirt

WENDY THE WEDDING PLANNER COZY MYSTERIES

Matrimony, Money and Murder

Chefs, Ceremonies and Crimes

Knives and Nuptials

Mice, Marriage and Murder

ABOUT THE AUTHOR

Cindy Bell is a USA Today and Wall Street Journal Bestselling Author. She is the author of the cozy mystery series Wagging Tail, Donut Truck, Dune House, Sage Gardens, Chocolate Centered, Macaron Patisserie, Nuts about Nuts, Bekki the Beautician, Heavenly Highland Inn and Wendy the Wedding Planner.

Cindy has always loved reading, but it is only recently that she has discovered her passion for writing romantic cozy mysteries. She loves walking along the beach thinking of the next adventure her characters can embark on.

You can sign up for her newsletter so you are notified of her latest releases at http://www.cindybellbooks.com.